THE CLASSMATE

WILL MCINTOSH

Future House Publishing

The Classmate

Future House Publishing

Cover illustration by Owen Richardson
Developmental editing by Anna Walker and Caylee Gardner
Substantive editing by James Dosdall
Copy editing by Mariah Madsen
Proofreading by Madison Rau
Interior design by Nicholas Baldwin

To Hannah and Miles, who like to remind me that I'm getting old, but keep me young.

CHAPTER 1

I'd never been on a quieter school bus. Kids were whispering to each other in tight, breathless tones as the bus clipped stray branches from the endless forest pressing in on either side of us.

"This isn't even a two-way road," I murmured to Lorena, the girl sitting beside me. When we'd loaded onto the bus in Annapolis, she'd dropped down beside me and just started talking. Normally I wasn't comfortable talking to people I didn't know—especially attractive girls my age—but Lorena had made it easy, keeping the conversation going for four hours, effortlessly filling in the awkward pauses I created. But even she had grown quieter when the bus had turned down this road.

Lorena peered out the window. "Where *is* this school? My folks told me this would be the greatest thing ever for my college application, but I don't know about this. This is freaky."

My mom had said the same thing. She'd said it was an educational program for the country's best and brightest. If it was successful, the government might expand it nationwide. She seemed to think the purpose of my entire childhood was to prepare me to get into a good college. I got as much say in this boarding school decision as I'd gotten when it came to competing on the neighborhood swim team, or attending math camp all last summer when all I'd wanted to do was decompress and play video games. Which was to say, I got no say.

Nothing I had said could change her mind. Dad, meanwhile, had been too busy bending over backward in his efforts to be liked by his new wife and stepchildren to even express an opinion about where I went to school.

The road was a jet black ribbon of blacktop that looked like it had been poured yesterday. The bus we were riding in, on the other hand, was old. My seat had a hole in the vinyl with foam bulging out of it. I plucked at the foam nervously.

"What do your parents do?" Lorena asked.

"Dad works for the power company. My mom's in

the CIA." Lorena looked impressed, so I added, "Don't picture someone in cool sunglasses traveling the world with a bunch of different aliases. She's a dork. She does data analysis." And what an argument I'd had with my dork mother over the phone. I still couldn't wrap my mind around that. Out of nowhere, she had convinced Dad to agree to pull me out of school and send me to a boarding school. Mom had said we couldn't refuse, given the *stakes*.

I was in *middle school.* My college applications six years from now? Is that what she considered high stakes? Probably.

"You said you don't see your mom much, right?" Lorena asked.

"Vacations, mostly. How about you, what do your parents do?"

The bus broke out of the trees so suddenly it startled me. The question forgotten, we peered out the window. A high, black, steel fence ran along the roadside like something out of a maximum-security prison. Up ahead, massive security gates swung open as we approached. I watched them shut behind us, fighting a rising claustrophobic panic.

Lorena pressed in beside me to get a better look. "What *is* this? Is this a school or a prison?"

The narrow strip of blacktop took us into a wide, flat field, but I could see the fence curving around us in the distance. Why would there be a huge security fence around a boarding school? New places made me nervous enough when they didn't have giant fences around them.

"Look at that!" a tall, skinny kid in the back of the bus called, pointing to my right.

We were passing beautifully landscaped brick walkways and gorgeous park areas with fountains and benches. I reached for my phone to snap a few photos, then remembered we hadn't been allowed to bring our phones. Because they interfered with your concentration. They distracted you from your academic pursuits. These were the same reasons I'd been given for why the school was in the middle of nowhere. All part of the plan to turbo-charge our young minds, if we didn't lose them first.

The wide, brick walkway was lined with shops, including an ice cream parlor and an arcade. That, I had not expected. At least there'd be something to do besides school. Still, this place was beyond weird.

We pulled onto a loop road that ringed a big oval lawn. On the other side of the lawn sat a one-story brown brick deal with evenly spaced windows along the front that screamed *middle school.*

As we got back in our seats, I wiped my clammy palms on my pants. Until now, I'd held it together pretty well, but the sight of the school had set my heart thrumming. I'd never been away from home, except for the occasional sleepover. And even those made me nervous. The truth was, everything made me nervous.

"Wait. Is that what it looks like?" An auburn-haired girl in a private school jacket was pointing over the rooftop of the three-story building to our left, where a cherry red track snaked high into the air. There was no mistaking it: it was the top of a roller coaster. Not a big job like you'd find at Busch Gardens, but more like something at a traveling carnival. Still, it was a roller coaster.

The bus squealed to a stop in front of a big building that looked like a town hall, with white pillars and wide concrete steps. The driver, a guy in his forties with a perfect haircut who looked nothing like a school bus driver, pointed. "Straight in those blue doors. Don't worry about your luggage—it'll be delivered to your dorm rooms."

My legs were shaking as I climbed down the steps of the bus behind Lorena. I half expected that now that we were off the bus, Lorena would wander off to find cooler kids to hang out with, but as we stepped off, she glanced back to make sure I was still there.

"I am freaking out right now," she said. "This place has *bad vibes*." She held her hands up, palms out, like she could feel them.

A woman with short silver hair wearing a gray suit stood waiting just inside the doors of the building, which was a wide-open atrium. She led us into a room filled with rows of seats, like in a movie theater. There was a packet on each seat. I wiped my sweaty palms and picked mine up.

An exhausted-looking woman giving us a big, enthusiastic smile stood at a podium up front. Her black hair was tied back so tightly it tugged the skin on her cheeks and the corners of her eyes.

"Welcome to Sagan Middle School. My name is Ms. Spain." She took a sip from a bottle of water. "You've been selected from thousands of students to take part in this unique program. What you learn here will change your lives and the lives of countless others."

I exchanged a look with Lorena. *Countless others?* Yes, I was sure we were going to change countless lives with our tireless pursuit of pre-algebra here at Sagan Middle School.

"Why don't we start with some of the basic rules?" Ms. Spain said. "Some of the rules will seem strange, but you *must* follow them if you want to complete the program successfully. Now open the envelope that was on your seat."

Ms. Spain told us to take out our earpieces, and she held one up so we could find ours in our envelopes. I located mine rolling around at the bottom. It was pea-sized and clear.

"Insert the earpiece into your left ear." She

demonstrated with the one she was holding.

I had no idea what this was about, but I did as I was told. The earpiece was small enough that it stuck down low.

"From this moment on, you are to keep the earpiece in your left ear at all times—even when you're sleeping," Ms. Spain said.

I looked over at Lorena, who gave me a look like, *Can you believe this?*

"Whenever a prompter says something to you through your earpiece, you are to immediately repeat it aloud." Ms. Spain held up a finger. "Unless the first word is *Direction* or *Do not repeat*. A *Direction* is something you are to do, not say. If your prompter begins with *Do not repeat*, he or she has something to say to you. If it's a question, answer out loud. Does everyone understand?"

Everyone nodded. No one was sticking the earpiece in their nose, or talking, or fidgeting in their seats. This was nothing like my school at home, which I already missed, even though I had not been particularly popular there. I reached for my phone, wanting to get a picture of this orientation to show to people when I got home, then remembered I didn't have it anymore.

"What the heck is going on?" Lorena was staring at her earbud, pinched between her thumb and finger.

The auburn-haired girl in the private school jacket shushed Lorena. Lorena glared over her shoulder at the girl. The look was clearly a warning not to shush her ever again.

I missed my phone. I wasn't sure I could go four phoneless months without having a complete mental breakdown.

"You've been chosen not just because you're intelligent, but also because of your maturity," Ms. Spain went on. "We're counting on that maturity." She paused and looked up and down the rows, making eye contact with each of us. "Tomorrow you'll meet a very special classmate. She looks different than you or anyone you've ever met. She—" Ms. Spain trailed off, trying to find the right words. "I'll be honest: you might find her frightening to look at. But it's important you don't stare. Treat her like any other student. Your prompters will guide you through the earbuds."

There was more about schedules and mealtimes, when we'd get to call home, and all of the fun we were going to have at the movie theater, the ice cream shop, and the carnival, but it was hard to concentrate, because the same words kept echoing in my head. *You might find her frightening to look at.*

What did *that* mean? Was she a burn victim? Did she have that elephant man disease where parts of her were horribly swollen? I didn't like this. From the looks on their faces, my new classmates didn't either.

I stopped in the doorway of my room, horrified. The room was lined with low, cot-like beds. Eight of them. No one had said anything about roommates, let alone *eight* of them. I'd been looking forward to having some alone time. At home, my bedroom was my refuge from my three stepsiblings, the place where I could relax and think my private thoughts in peace.

Lorena squeezed past me. "Ooh! Dibs on the window!" She ran toward the bed closest to the window and leaped onto it, bouncing. She stretched out, cradled her head in her palms, and let out a satisfied sigh.

Coed? The dorms were *coed?* I wasn't going to survive this place. As a few other kids passed me, I raced to claim the bed closest to Lorena. If I was going to share a room with seven other people, I was at least going to sleep near the one person I knew. I took a seat on the bed to claim it and looked around what would be my bedroom for the next four months. There were paintings on the wall that you might see in a hotel room—a beach scene, a farmhouse seen through a picket fence, an abstract with a lot of purple. As I sat there, it occurred to me that I was probably sharing a bathroom with a bunch of people as well. This was a nightmare.

"This is pretty sweet!" a stocky, baby-faced guy two beds down and across from me said, staring at the ceiling from his bed. He sat up. "Hey, we should organize a touch football game on that field in front of the school."

A couple of the other people in the room seemed interested. I acted like I hadn't heard him.

Lorena sprang up. "We should take turns telling creepy stories after lights out!"

"*No*," a thin girl whose bed was close to the door said. "I don't want to be up all night,"

I was pretty sure I was going to be up all night either way.

CHAPTER 2

I headed into the cafeteria, my hair still wet from showering, and looked around for a place to sit. The prospect of plunking down among a group of kids I didn't know made me wildly uncomfortable.

A waving hand caught my attention—it was Lorena, sitting at an otherwise empty table in the corner by the window. Relieved, I hurried over.

Lorena gave me a big smile. "How's it going?" She was clearly a morning person, no sign of sleepiness in her brown eyes.

"Okay, I guess." That was all the enthusiasm I could muster at eight a.m.

The cafeteria was like a restaurant. There were waiters

to take your order, and they had everything—pancakes, eggs cooked to order, French toast, Cocoa Puffs, frozen yogurt, anything you could think of. It was cool, but I also found it a little creepy. What sort of school has *waiters*?

Lorena had ordered everything, or just about. She had three plates in front of her. She caught me gawking at her breakfast and stopped mid-chew.

"What?"

"Nothing. It's just . . . you've got an amazing appetite."

She forked another hunk of blueberry pancakes into her mouth. "I know. I always eat like this. I must have an incredible metabolism."

I, on the other hand, didn't have much appetite when I was in strange, new places. I picked at my chocolate chip pancakes, each bit feeling like it was clinging to the sides of my throat on the way down.

Lorena was studying me. "You okay? Don't take this the wrong way, but you seem, like, way tense."

I laughed. I had a nervous laugh that came braying out sometimes when nothing was funny. "I'm always way tense. I have an anxiety disorder. Being sent to a strange boarding school on two days' notice definitely doesn't help it."

"What is an anxiety disorder, exactly? I mean, I've heard of it, obviously. But I don't totally get it."

"It's just . . . you feel anxious a lot of the time." I

felt uncomfortable saying too much about it. I wanted Lorena to understand why I seemed "way tense," but I didn't really want to dwell on it.

Lorena leaned in closer. "But *why*? What causes it?"

"The way my psychologist explained it, my anxiety volume button is broken, basically. We all have a baseline level of anxiety. If you have low baseline anxiety, you mostly get anxious if there's a good reason, like you have to give a speech in front of a bunch of people, or you're going to have surgery. Then there are people like me. Most mornings I wake up feeling like I'm going to have to give a speech and *then* have surgery."

Most kids I told looked embarrassed for me, or uncomfortable. Lorena looked genuinely concerned, which was a nice change. I felt so lucky we'd ended up sitting together on the bus ride in. Lorena was so easy to talk to. She was good at filling awkward silences, which were my specialty.

"Is there anything that can fix it?" she asked.

I shrugged. "My psychologist helps a little. Medication helps. But I still spend most of my time feeling anxious."

"That sucks."

Another student stopped at our table. She was African American, her head nearly shaved, freckles running across the bridge of her nose. She was small, but everyone was supposed to be in seventh grade, so she must have just been small for her age. She had an intense expression—not angry, but no smile in sight.

"Have a seat," Lorena said, gesturing. "We've got tons of room." Which is what you're supposed to say to make someone feel welcome.

Me, I just sat there saying nothing, feeling awkward in the presence of a new face. I was disappointed someone had broken up our table for two. I felt more comfortable talking to one person at a time, where I knew when it was my turn to speak and didn't have to try to jump in when there was a pause. Plus, Lorena was the only person I sort of knew here. I didn't want to lose the one friend I had or end up as the tagalong like I usually did.

A waiter came over to take the new girl's order. The girl ordered all healthy stuff—fruit, yogurt, whole-grain waffle.

"Have either of you heard anything from your earbud yet?" she asked as the waiter walked off. "I haven't heard squat from mine."

"Me neither," Lorena said.

I just shook my head. The earbud was uncomfortable. It partially blocked my ear canal, making sounds louder in one ear than the other. It also made me feel strangely off-balance.

Lorena stuck out her hand. "I'm Lorena, by the way."

"Persephone."

"Benjamin," I mumbled. Persephone stuck out her hand, and we shook as well.

"I don't understand what they're going to use them for," Persephone said. "We're in school, but some stranger is going to tell us what to *say?*"

"Maybe they can feed us answers on our tests," I ventured as I poured more syrup on my chocolate chip pancakes so they'd go down more easily.

Lorena chuckled at my joke and went back to fueling up. "So where are you from?" she asked Persephone.

"Baltimore."

"A city girl. And it goes without saying that you're exceptionally mature, or you wouldn't be here," Lorena joked.

Persephone gave a sharp, harsh laugh. "I'm exceptionally *something.*"

The bell rang. Everyone started filing out of the cafeteria.

"Well, here we go." Lorena took a deep breath.

Persephone fell into step beside us as we filed out. She was wearing all black—t-shirt, loose pants, tennis shoes.

We cut through a gate and headed across the center courtyard, toward the school.

Persephone pointed as we walked. "You can see more of those carnival rides from here."

The roller coaster had a big sign on it with *Cyclone* in yellow lettering. There was a high corkscrew drop at the end. Beside The Cyclone was a Ferris wheel, then one of those ships that swung back and forth, an alpine sled ride, and then a row of game booths.

"I wonder if we'll get to ride them," Lorena said. "I've never been on a roller coaster."

"You've never been to Great Escape, or Busch Gardens?" I asked.

Lorena threw her hands in the air. "I've never been *anywhere*."

"They said we wouldn't need money while we're here," Persephone said. "Either that means the rides are free, or we aren't going to get to ride them."

"That would stink to have carnival rides sitting right there and not get to ride them," Lorena said as we reached our new school.

The doors to Sagan Middle School were propped wide open. Despite the school-like appearance of the outside, the inside was weird. It had no metal detectors, no security guard. There were no lockers in the hallway, just freshly painted white walls. The strange empty building gave me a crawling sensation, but I got that feeling in all strange new places, and sometimes in familiar old places as well.

"What do you think the deal is with this special student?" Persephone asked. "Her appearance might *scare* us? What does that even mean?"

"*Direction*," a man's voice said through my earpiece, startling me. "Change the topic. Talk about something pleasant—how good breakfast was or a recent movie you saw."

I could tell from Lorena's and Persephone's expressions that they'd just gotten their first earbud direction as well and they were also disturbed to realize people were listening in on our conversation.

"Okay then." Lorena cleared her throat. "This place is going to be fun. How about those Packers?"

"Read any good books lately?" Persephone said, grinning, as we headed into the classroom.

I slowed as I stepped through the doorway.

It was taking up two seats pushed together. It was bluish and lumpy with all of these folds, and, *oh man*, were those her *eyes* or her *ears*? She was wearing a purple dress and weird round patent leather shoes, and a bow was in her hair, only it wasn't hair, it was more like black spaghetti, and I couldn't breathe.

The thing in the seats *flexed*, and suddenly it wasn't lumpy anymore—it was hard and sharp, with pointy barbs sticking out of it. It hissed like a giant punctured tire.

"*Direction*," the man's voice said through my earpiece. "Do not stare. Put a smile on your face, find your seat, and face the board."

Panting, shaking, I looked at the name cards tented on the desks, searching for my name. When I finally spotted it, my insides felt like they were turning to water.

My seat was right next to the thing.

"Direction. Take a deep breath and sit *down*," the earpiece voice said. "Do not repeat. She won't hurt you."

Pressing my hands on desktops to stay upright as I passed, I slid into my seat and leaned as far away from the thing as I could, the muscles in my neck so tight I heard a creak when I turned to look at the board.

I could hear it breathing beside me—a hiss like a bicycle tire inflating and deflating. I couldn't get those ear-eyes out of my mind. The jet black dots darting around in the centers must have been its eyes, but they were surrounded by thick, dark purple folds and ridges that resembled the outsides of ears. It had no neck, just a wide purple head attached right to its massive torso.

A few kids gasped as they filed into the room, but I didn't look—I kept my eyes on the board as I'd been instructed. That voice knew what was going on, and I didn't, so I was going to do exactly what it said.

The teacher, a middle-aged woman with dark, curly hair breezed into the room with a bright smile on her face. She acted like there was nothing strange going on, welcomed us to the school, introduced herself as Ms. Bazzini, and started taking attendance. When she called my name, I said, "Here," in a tight squeak that barely made it out of my throat.

Then she called "Eve" and looked to my right at the beast. Ms. Bazzini raised her eyebrows, encouraging "Eve."

Out of the corner of my eye, I saw the thing tentatively raise a fingerless hand. Ms. Bazzini beamed and nodded. She called the next name.

What *was* this thing? I wanted so badly to bolt from my seat and climb over that fence and keep running until I was safe in my room, under my blanket. I made eye contact with Lorena, who was leaning off the edge of her seat to be as far away from it as she could, even though she was on the other side of the room.

"*Wow*," she mouthed silently.

"Direction. Eyes front," Earbud Guy said. I turned to face front and looked around for the camera this guy was using to see my every move. I couldn't find it.

Someone near the back of the room was crying quietly. I glanced back. It was a kid with bushy brown hair named Drew, who slept in my dorm room.

There was no math, no science. A ton of recent history, a little English, and then . . . etiquette. *Etiquette.* There was no such class in school as etiquette. We learned how to make polite conversation—how to keep the tone positive and constructive, how to find something to compliment about the other person. Ms. Bazzini went on and on about the proper way to greet someone you're meeting for the first time. How old did she think we were? Four? We knew how to greet someone.

"Now I want you to pair up and practice this," Ms. Bazzini said.

My heart hammering, I turned and tapped the big kid sitting to my left on the shoulder. "Want to be partners?" But Ms. Bazzini was going down the rows, pointing with forked fingers, calling out pairs of names, and as she came down my row, I could see who those forked fingers were going to pair me with.

"Ben and Eve . . ."

My lips went numb. My fingertips too. There was no way I could use them to shake this monster's hand. I wanted to cry, or scream. I wanted my mother. But more than anything, I wanted to *run*.

"Do not repeat," Earbud Guy said. "Here we go, Ben. This may be hard to believe, but she's as nervous as you are. Stand up and face her."

I didn't want to—I so, so didn't want to—but I did what the voice said, because that's what you do; you do what adults tell you, especially in school.

The creature went on staring straight ahead.

"Hi, my name is Ben," Earbud Guy said.

It took me a moment to remember I was supposed to repeat that. I opened my crater-dry mouth and said, "Hi, my name is Ben."

The creature turned her head ever so slightly.

"This is a stupid exercise, isn't it?" the voice prompted.

I repeated it.

The creature ignored me.

"It's good to meet you anyway, Eve," the voice said.

"Direction. Now extend your hand and offer to shake."

There was no way I was going to do that. I'd seen the way barbs could come stabbing out of this thing. The words I could say, though.

"It's good to meet you anyway, Eve."

I turned to sit.

"Direction," the voice nearly shouted. "Now offer her your hand. Don't let me down here, Ben."

I hesitated. The voice was like an invisible hand, pushing me, turning me. I didn't want to do this, I *so* didn't want to.

I stuck out my trembling hand.

Eve looked at it, then away.

I went to drop my hand, but Earbud Guy jumped in. "Direction. Keep it there."

I stood there with my hand in the air, trembling from head to toe. Everyone in the room was watching, while trying not to make it obvious, probably getting directions from their earbud voices telling them not to stare.

Eve raised her hand, or hoof, or whatever it was, without looking at me. I looked down at the fat stump of purple flesh.

"Do not repeat. *Yes. Good,*" Earbud Guy shouted. "Her fingers are about four inches up her arm. See them?"

I nodded. There were four of them, writhing around like they had minds of their own.

"Don't nod. Grasp two of the fingers, *very* gently, and shake them once."

I was panting like I'd just run a marathon as I grasped what looked like two purplish worms, shook the mushy, jiggly things for a split second, then brought my hand back and lunged into my seat.

"Do not repeat. Nice work, Ben. Nice, nice work." In the background, I thought I could hear other voices, just barely. They sounded like they were cheering.

My heart slowed as relief washed over me. I'd survived.

What kind of school *was* this?

As Ms. Bazzini went on about formal versus informal greetings, I looked over at Lorena, but she didn't notice. She was busy being in shock, staring glassy eyed at the board. Persephone, on the other hand, caught my eye and gave me a knowing smile, like she was somehow *enjoying* this. I was not. I felt as if Eve might turn at any minute and take a bite out of my face. I fixed my gaze on the dry-erase board and tried to forget what was sitting beside me. After class, if I survived, I'd ask one of the adults in this loony bin if I could switch seats.

CHAPTER 3

Usually the second night in a strange place is easier than the first, but this place felt worse than it had the night before. As I lay in bed staring out through the window at the black sky, I was sure I was never going to sleep again, because if I did, I might dream of Eve's fingers.

"This is so screwed up," Lorena said from the bed next to mine.

"Yep." I waited anxiously for Earbud Guy to cut in and tell me to change the conversation, but he was silent.

"This is a test of some sort." Persephone was lying flat on the bed to my left, looking up at the ceiling. The kids at the other end of the room were whispering urgently to each other, probably having the same conversation as us.

"What do you mean?" I asked.

"It's faked somehow. To test how we respond."

"I *promise* you, she's not fake." I'd touched her. I would know.

"Been to the movies lately?" Persephone asked. "You can create incredibly lifelike effects if you have the money."

Could she be fake? Could Eve be a guy inside a costume, the spines remote control? That was hard to imagine. But what explanation for Eve *wasn't* far-fetched?

"She has to be an alien," I said. "Either from another planet or pulled from an alternate dimension." I'd read and watched enough science fiction to recognize an alien when I saw one.

"And they decided the thing to do was put the alien in a classroom with a bunch of seventh graders and teach her how to shake hands properly." Persephone's voice dripped sarcasm. "That makes perfect sense. I'm telling you, *we're* the subjects in this experiment."

"It's not an experiment." Lorena was still sitting on the edge of her bed in her sweats. "I don't think she's an alien, though."

Persephone sat up on her elbows. "There's a third possibility? Okay. What do *you* think she is?"

"Whatever name you want to give her, she's not something you can explain with science." Lorena hesitated, like she wanted to say more, but was afraid we'd laugh.

"Like what?" I prodded.

"Can't you recognize a supernatural being when you see one? Someone was screwing around with ancient knowledge they didn't understand—probably the government—and Eve is the result."

Persephone squeezed her eyes shut. "Please tell me you're not suggesting Eve is some sort of demon."

I looked to Lorena. I had never believed in the supernatural, but after walking into that classroom this morning and seeing Eve, I was open to rethinking my beliefs.

"Just *look at her*," Lorena said, "I'm telling you, she was summoned."

Persephone made a sound in the back of her throat. "Once again, if the government caught a *demon*, would they put it in with a bunch of seventh graders and teach it the proper way to greet strangers? How does that make sense?"

She had a point.

"*None* of this makes sense," Lorena half whispered, half shouted. "But that is not a man in a costume."

"I promise you, it is," Persephone said.

There was a knock on the open door. Ms. Spain stepped into our room, still dressed in a dark gray business suit with her hair pulled back. She looked over her shoulder. "Come on, it's okay."

Eve appeared in the doorway, wearing green and

white striped silk pajamas.

"Here you go." Ms. Spain patted the empty bed, the one closest to the door.

My vision went totally black for a moment as my thumping heart went into overdrive. A small, terrified sound escaped one of the kids' lips as Eve stepped into the room and stood facing the bed.

"Is there anything you need?" Ms. Spain asked Eve.

Eve didn't answer.

"Well, I'll let you get some sleep." Ms. Spain turned to the rest of us. "Good night, everyone."

No. Just, no. They wouldn't leave us alone all night in the dark with this thing, would they? I exchanged a panicked look with Lorena. When I glanced at Persephone, she just shrugged. I guess if it really was a guy in a suit, there was nothing to worry about.

Eve sat on the edge of her bed, the springs creaking loudly. Lucian McQue was gaping, wide-eyed, from his spot three beds away from her, his blanket pulled up to his nose. Drew, the kid who'd been crying in class, had retreated completely under his blanket. Alyssa, the girl sleeping closest to Eve, had her eyes squeezed shut, pretending she was sleeping. That wasn't a bad idea. I closed my eyes, as far from sleep as I'd ever been in my life.

At the other end of the room, the springs in Eve's bed creaked some more as she lay down.

I wanted to go home, right now. I wanted to be in my own bed, alone in my own room, in my house on Mason Drive.

"I have to go to the *bathroom*," Lorena whispered.

I glanced at Eve, her huge body filling the whole bed.

"Just go," I said uncertainly.

Lorena didn't move. I couldn't blame her—she'd have to walk past Eve. When I was a kid, I always felt like a hand or something might dart out from under the bed and grab my ankle when I got up to go to the bathroom in the dark. Here, the monster wasn't under the bed, it was *in* the bed.

Still, Lorena couldn't hold it all night. "I shook her hand. It's okay."

Lorena swung back the blankets and sat up. She sat there for a long time before finally standing and padding toward the door.

As she approached Eve's bed, Eve hissed. Even in the semi-darkness I could see her harden in silhouette, the barbs popping up on her skin like weaponized goose bumps.

Lorena squealed and raced back to her bed, yanking the blankets over her head.

How could we possibly sleep with a monster in the room? How could we even close our eyes? I lay staring at the stucco ceiling, wishing I was home in my own comfy bed.

From the other side of the long room, Eve let out a soft foghorn rumble—a strange, otherworldly sound that rose and fell. It took me a moment to notice the words mixed in with those sounds. "Don't come near me . . . hurt you . . . I can. I can hurt you bad . . ."

I rolled to face the window, pulling the blanket over my head, hoping it really was just a man in a suit. And hoping just as hard that Lorena was wrong, that this was not a demon sleeping in the room with us.

CHAPTER 4

Six kids were lined up behind me outside the old-fashioned phone booth set in front of the ice cream shop, including Grace Krivitzky, still wearing her private school jacket, and tall, gangly Jacob Warnock. Seems I wasn't the only kid who needed to hear a familiar voice this morning. I was so tired. I'd finally dozed off at around four a.m., then had a nightmare and was awake by six.

As I dialed, Earbud Guy spoke. "Direction. Do not refer to Eve, directly or indirectly, during your call."

Did that mean Mom didn't know about Eve? Maybe I'd been sent here under false pretenses. It would be comforting to think Mom hadn't known what she was getting me into.

Mom answered on the first ring. "Hi, Benny. How are you?"

My throat tightened. I was seriously afraid I was going to start crying, which would be humiliating with a line of kids watching. In a voice strangled with emotion, I said, "Not so good."

There was a pause. "You can do this, Benny. It'll . . . it'll get better."

"Better?" I made the word sound like it left a bitter taste in my mouth. "Well, I guess it can't get worse."

"Be brave. You can do this."

Be *brave*? Maybe she did know about Eve. Was it possible she'd sent me here knowing I'd be attending classes with . . . whatever Eve was?

A jolt of adrenaline raced through me as I spotted Eve crossing the street. She was clutching an oversized soda and wearing a Wonder Woman t-shirt. I pressed against the glass, trying to make myself as small as possible as Eve passed within a few feet of the phone booth. She kept walking, not giving me the slightest glance. Thank goodness. Just the sight of her terrified me. I dreaded going to class in a few minutes.

"*How could you send me here?*" I blurted. "This is a *nightmare*."

Mom didn't answer for a long time. When she did, I could tell she was crying. My mother never cried. "It's that bad?"

Earbud Guy spoke. "I guess it's not *that* bad. I'm just really homesick."

I stood there holding the phone to my ear, my mouth hanging open. He wanted me to repeat words he fed me to my own *mother?*

"Direction," Earbud Guy said. "Repeat what I just said, immediately. 'I guess it's not that bad. I'm just really homesick.'"

"I guess it's not that bad. I'm just really homesick," I repeated in a monotone.

Mom sounded relieved. "You'll get over that in no time. You'll make friends, and pretty soon you won't want to come home."

I doubted that. I sincerely doubted that.

"I've already made two friends, actually," Earbud Guy said.

"I've already made two friends, actually," I repeated.

"And the food here is amazing," Earbud Guy said. "There's even an amusement park."

I repeated the words, although with far less enthusiasm than Earbud Guy.

"An amusement park?" Mom said. "You've got to be kidding me. Have you called your dad yet? I'm sure he's eager to know how you're doing."

"Eager" seemed like an overstatement. Sometimes I felt as if my dad saw me as baggage from his past that he was embarrassed about.

"Not yet," I said.

I repeated the words Earbud Guy told me to say until he told me to say goodbye. As I hung up, I wondered what the point of calling home was if you didn't get to choose your own words.

"Do not repeat. If you want to keep your phone privileges, you need to follow the rules, Benjamin," Earbud Guy said.

"I didn't say anything about Eve. I just asked how she could send me here."

"You implied something was amiss," Earbud Guy said, as if there wasn't something amiss.

I walked past the line of kids waiting for their turn to use the phone. "Does my mother know about Eve?" I asked Earbud Guy.

Earbud Guy didn't answer. *I'm just very homesick*, he'd made me tell my mother. Yes, I was homesick. I was also scared out of my mind. I was afraid I might die here.

Be Brave, Mom had said. If she knew what was going on here, then all I had to say to her was, *that's easy for you to say in your warm, safe home two hundred miles from Eve.*

CHAPTER 5

I picked up one of the smooth stones that filled the spaces between the thousands of tulips growing in the courtyard where Lorena, Persephone, and I sat on a forest green park bench. The bench was spotless, as if it had come straight out of a package and was placed here yesterday. Everything at Sagan Middle School seemed brand new.

"You can't grow tulips in the fall," Persephone said.

"What do you mean?" I asked, looking out at a sea of tulips.

"It's a spring flower. They don't bloom in fall."

I shrugged. Just one more mystery. Compared to Eve, it seemed like a small one.

Lorena was examining a cut along the side of her

index finger. It was long, but not too deep.

"What did you do?" I asked.

"Didn't you hear? Eve smashed all of the mirrors in the girls' bathroom." She said it matter-of-factly, as if people smashed mirrors all the time. "I was trying to hold up one of the bigger pieces so I could see to brush my hair."

"This place is so messed up." Persephone was monkeying with some sort of round electronic device about the size of a golf ball. She had a panel open and was dissecting it with a miniature screwdriver and tweezers.

"What's that?" I asked.

"One of their surveillance cameras," she answered.

I nearly jumped. "*What?* Where did you get it?"

Persephone stopped working. "In the dorm. Inside the ceiling tile over our beds."

Lorena threw back her head and laughed. "That is *sick*. You go, girl."

"Aren't you going to get in trouble?" I asked.

Persephone shrugged. "Not so far. I mean, I'm assuming they know it was me, since this is a camera." She was an interesting mix, her big eyes and baby face offset by her shaved head and utter lack of fear.

"Why are you taking it apart?" I asked.

She went back to monkeying with the surveillance camera. "What you understand, you control. What you don't understand, controls you. If I'm going to have a phone with me every minute of my life, I want to know everything about it, from how it works on an electronic level, to what's happening when I visit a website. Google, Snapchat, Microsoft, *none* of them get any information about me. When I'm online, *I'm* the one who gets information."

Wow. I barely knew how to change the battery in my phone. I was a little intimidated by Persephone's self-assurance, by how far ahead of me she seemed to be in figuring out the world. And I was intimidated by how easy Lorena was around people, and how flat-out gorgeous she was, with her exotic almond-shaped eyes and perfect cheekbones. My stepsister Ruby said you shouldn't be influenced by people's appearance, that it was the least important thing about them, but I couldn't help it. Beautiful girls intimidated me even more than other people did.

"Do you think our parents know that *very special student* is here?" Persephone asked, sarcastically using the phrase Ms. Spain had used to describe Eve in our orientation.

I shifted on the bench. We'd been sitting here long enough that the slats were getting uncomfortable. "The way she acted on the phone, I think my mom knows *something's* going on."

Persephone set the camera on the bench. "I seriously doubt mine does. She made me sit in a booster seat in our minivan until I was twelve, and last year when we went on a cruise, she tried to make me wear a life preserver whenever I was on the deck. She never would have sent me if she knew what was here. I'm still surprised she let me go at all, but my father insisted. My mother usually wins those sorts of standoffs, but not this time."

It was odd how the three of us had latched on to each other so quickly. A lot of the other kids were forming their own groups. Being scared to death probably had a lot to do with how fast we were bonding.

Persephone checked her watch. "How long do you think they'll let us stay out here?"

"Hopefully till it's time to go home," Lorena said.

We'd come straight from dinner, figuring it was as far from Eve as we could get. During dinner Eve had shouted at people to stop looking at her. The way she stuck her face in her plate and sucked up food with her huge, lipless mouth made it hard for some students to look away. Personally, the sight of Eve eating made me nauseous. I had no problem looking away.

"I miss my friends," Lorena said.

"Me too," Persephone agreed.

When I didn't say anything, Lorena gave me a questioning look.

"I guess I miss them."

"You *guess*." Lorena studied me. "What are you not saying?"

"It's just, I tend to be on the fringe of things."

"Meaning?" Lorena prodded.

I considered how to put it. "I'm the one they call as an afterthought, or who they invite along because I happen to be standing there when they're making plans. I'm never the 'best friend.' When I was younger, I used to fantasize about having a best friend. I'd imagine us having sleepovers, playing video games, and going to movies together. At home, I usually go to movies with my dad and stepmom and stepsiblings."

"Do you get along with them? Your stepsiblings?" Persephone asked.

"They're mostly fine. But the three of them have known each other their entire lives, so I'm kind of a sixth wheel in my own family. And I'm quiet. A lot of the time, I just blend into the background."

"Aww." Lorena jutted out her bottom lip. "That hurts my heart." She opened her arms and gave me a big hug. "Well, now you have a best friend. After this is over, I promise I'll keep in touch."

"Make that two best friends," Persephone said. Had it really been just a few days ago that I'd resented Persephone joining our table for breakfast? I was glad she had.

Earbud Guy cut in. "There's a special party in Jubilation Hall starting in ten minutes. It's an eight-minute walk, so you'd better get going."

Persephone stood. "Jubilation Hall? What kind of a name is that?"

"A lame one." Lorena stood as well. "I sure hope there aren't any mirrors in Jubilation Hall."

Persephone headed off toward Jubilation Hall, leading the way. She stopped suddenly. "What if we don't go?"

"What do you mean?" I asked.

"What happens if we don't go? There don't seem to be any punishments here. No one's ever said, 'If you don't follow the rules, you'll be confined to your room, or you won't get to see the movie,' or whatever. Don't you think that's weird?"

"I can name some weirder things about this place, right off the top of my head," Lorena said.

"Remember what Ms. Spain said during orientation?" I said. "Part of the reason we were selected is because we're good kids. They're probably assuming they won't *need* to punish us."

"I guess," Persephone said. She didn't sound convinced. But as Lorena and I continued to walk forward, she followed us.

We headed toward Jubilation Hall, feeling not the least bit jubilant.

CHAPTER 6

The lights went out, and the strobe light came on again. Kids waved their arms. The kids on the dance floor did crazy dance moves to get the full effect. Lucian, the big guy who had tried to organize a football game on the quad, was running around like a puppy who'd lapped up a pitcher of coffee. He put his heart and soul into anything his prompter told him to do. My guess was, the prompter was the closest thing there was to a coach here.

"Direction. Move around. Get out there and dance," Earbud Guy said. Except I wasn't a fun-haver in that way. I felt more comfortable hanging out on the periphery.

Persephone waved one hand in the air, putting in the absolute minimum amount of effort possible after her own prompter had goaded her to "move around." That seemed like the way to go, so I joined her.

Out of our crew, only Lorena was dancing, and I was certain that was only because she liked to dance and always seemed to have a ton of energy trying to burst out of her.

"What *is* this?" I was completely mesmerized by the whole spectacle.

"It's incredibly artificial, incredibly pretentious fun," Persephone said.

Grace, who was wearing a black dress instead of her ubiquitous private school jacket, came toward our little group, clapping, and did a cheerleader leg kick. "Come on, pump it up!" She reminded me so much of my mother, with her gangly build, knobby knees, and relentless drive to never get an answer wrong.

We ignored her. Ever since Grace had shushed Lorena during the orientation, there'd been tension between our little tribes.

Eve was on the opposite side of the big hall, sitting at her own table, hissing at anyone who wandered too close. She didn't look like she was having much fun either.

The song ended, and the party emcee, or whatever he was, jogged up onto the stage and grabbed the microphone. "Okay, time for our next door prize. Everyone got their tickets?"

A bunch of people cheered or waved their tickets.

One thing I had to say for this party, the prizes they were giving out were incredible.

"This one is for a brand-new Xbox Gold." He held the Xbox in the air. An Xbox. They were giving away a freaking Xbox.

The emcee raised the crazy purple sunglasses he was wearing to go with his crazy purple outfit and top hat. He pressed a button on the electronic screen behind him, and a virtual wheel began to spin like a slot machine.

"Who will it be?" the emcee shouted.

The wheel slowed and stopped on 886.

It was my number.

Stunned, I ran toward the stage as people cheered, no doubt prompted by their earbuds.

The emcee checked my ticket. "Our winner is Benjamin! Let's give him a big hand!" He pressed the Xbox into my hands. The shrink-wrap felt cool against my palms. I raised it in the air and carried it back to my friends as the applause petered out. I'd won an Xbox. I'd begged for one for Christmas, but it had been too expensive for Dad, and Mom thought video games rotted your brain and didn't build character or add to your *résumé*. I'd have to keep it out of her sight or she'd confiscate it.

"The grand prize drawing is in a few minutes," the emcee said. "Who's going to win that incredibly cool ride?"

I glanced at the three-wheeled, Harley-Davidson, custom Star Wars–themed chopper motorcycle sitting in the middle of the floor. It was a black, glistening, highly polished miracle. It had a governor installed that limited the rider to fifteen miles per hour, but still, it was a motorcycle.

"Well, they bought Benjamin off." Persephone eyed my Xbox. "They can count on his complete obedience now."

"No, they can't," I protested.

"Yes, they can. This is what the powerful do—they throw just enough crumbs at the masses to make them feel grateful for their chains."

I squinted at Persephone. She was one strange kid. She looked like she was nine, but she talked like a college professor. I would never say it out loud, but I wondered how she got picked for this program, since the teachers were so hyper-focused on everyone following the rules, and Persephone was the exact opposite of a rule follower.

Out in the center of the floor, Lucian did a handstand, then lifted one hand off the floor so he was holding his entire body up with one hand. Earbud Guy instructed me to applaud. I clapped twice.

"Who decided you had to be athletic to be cool?" Persephone asked.

I had no idea. At the moment, I didn't really care.

The emcee hopped up onto the stage. "It's time." He

raised his hands in the air and clapped, encouraging us to join in. "That's right—it's time to give away the grand prize." The lights went out; a spotlight painted the Star Wars chopper in bright light, making it glimmer like a jewel. "One of you is going to be cruising around campus in style tomorrow. Who will it be?"

"Please let it be me," Lucian cried out, shaking his clasped hands in the air.

The emcee raised a finger. "The wheel of chance will decide. Ready?"

A dozen voices shouted yes.

"All right. Here we go." The emcee activated the wheel. It spun for an extra-long time before ticking to a stop on number 483.

"Who has four eighty-three?" The emcee scanned the audience. I'd expected someone to shout out immediately, but the silence stretched on. The spotlight swung around the room, seeking the winner. "Someone must have the winning number. Don't be shy; call it out, or raise your hand. Four, eight, three."

The spotlight painted kid after kid, searching. It passed over Eve, then circled back. Eve's fingerless arm was raised.

"We have a winner!" the emcee shouted. "Eve is our grand prize winner."

There was dead silence in the room.

"Direction. Clap," Earbud Guy said. "Come on, give

her a hand."

I clapped. Other kids joined in.

"Direction. *Harder*," Earbud Guy said. "Come on, make it loud."

The applause got louder and louder. A few kids threw in a whoop, no doubt at the direction of their prompters.

"Congratulations, *Eve*." the emcee gestured toward the chopper. "Go ahead, try it out."

Eve lowered her raised arm. She seemed confused.

The emcee gestured more emphatically. "Go on."

Eve, who was wearing an orange dress with white trim, stalked over to the motorcycle, her big, round hooflike feet thudding on the polished wood floor. She swung her leg over the seat. She gripped the handlebars.

"Twist the left for gas, the right for break," the emcee said.

"Wait," I said, "he's going to let her ride it *in here?*"

Before I'd finished the sentence, Eve was off. She cruised around the floor as kids hustled to get out of her way. It seemed like an incredibly dangerous thing to do. At my middle school at home, we weren't allowed to *run* in the halls for fear we might skin a knee, let alone ride a motorcycle.

Eve let out a wheezy, triumphant cough that must have been her version of laughter. She veered to the left, then the right, then made a big circle as trumpet-heavy music boomed.

"How stupid do they think we are?" Persephone said in my ear.

I shrugged at her. "What do you mean?"

Lorena leaned in to hear what we were talking about.

"The drawing was obviously rigged," Persephone said, her eyebrows pinched. "This whole school is about Eve, so of *course* she wins the grand prize. She probably doesn't even really win it. Whoever is playing Eve gives it back after the experiment is over."

"It's not a guy in a suit," I said.

"And she just happened to win the grand prize fair and square?"

I hesitated, watching Eve tool around Jubilation Hall. "I think you're probably right about that. It was rigged."

"What about *you* winning?" Lorena gestured toward the Xbox. "Do you think that was random?"

I hadn't even considered that. I looked down at my brand-new Xbox. Had I won it as a bribe to buy my obedience, like Persephone said?

"I don't know."

The double doors swung open. People began filing out, heading back to the dorm.

Eve turned her chopper toward the exit, riding right past us.

"Congratulations, Eve. You are so lucky!" Earbud Guy prompted me.

"Congratulations, Eve. You are so lucky!" I dutifully shouted. I wasn't sure if she heard me over the rumble of the chopper. If she did, she ignored me.

We lagged behind the others and paused to sit in a gorgeous courtyard, where water cascaded down a mini-waterfall under the starlight. Everyone called it the Niagara Courtyard.

It had taken a few days to get to know the layout, but I had a good idea where everything was by now. In the center was the quad, a grassy oval the size of a football field, which was surrounded by the school, the dorm, and the cafeteria. A wide, brick walkway lined with ornate lampposts wound from the quad past an ice cream shop, a candy store, a movie theater, and an arcade. All the things a thirteen-year-old could want. We called that part of the compound Main Street. If you followed it to the end, you reached the amusement park, which had six rides and a bunch of carnival games we could play for free.

The other direction, where we were now, was a maze of brick walkways winding around a half dozen buildings. There were little parks between the buildings, with benches and shady gardens. One park was filled with thousands and thousands of tulips in a rainbow of colors, and we called that Tulipville. Another had a little bridge that crossed over a pond filled with lily pads. The biggest one had a huge, tiered fountain with dozens of life-sized Star Wars character statues frozen in battle poses. Rey was perched on the highest tier, a gusher of water shooting from her lightsaber. The edges of Star Wars Park, as we called it, were lined with statues of other characters, along with fifteen- to twenty-foot-tall models of the *Millennium Falcon* and the Death Star.

Lorena held out her hands and flipped them from palms up to palms down and back again. "Now, this spot has good qi."

"Good what?" I asked.

"Good qi. Good energy. My great-grandma was a shaman in Honduras. She taught me some things."

"Is that your mom's grandmother?" Persephone asked.

Lorena nodded. "Dad's from Mexico. He and my mom met in a chicken factory. One of those romantic stories Hollywood's always making movies about."

"Right." Persephone turned to me. "How about you? Where are your roots?"

"Mostly Poland on my mom's side. My dad's parents immigrated from Ireland. Most of them worked in the coal mines in Pennsylvania. Mom and Dad met in the army. Mom stayed on. Dad did his four years and went to work for the power company back home."

Lorena turned her head toward the dark sky. "Too bad we can't sleep out here under the stars. The dorm room has bad qi."

"I would think so, what with a demon sleeping there." Persephone nudged Lorena.

"Speaking of which." I jerked my thumb in the direction of the dorm. "We should head back before our earbud overlords kick us out."

"Nah. Let's stay until they make us go," Lorena said.

That seemed like a better idea. I leaned back on the bench and soaked in the qi.

CHAPTER 7

I looked up and down the hall. No sign of Persephone. There was a buzzing coming from the girls' bathroom. I leaned close to the door. "Persephone?"

The door swung open. Persephone was shaving her head with an electric razor. Behind her, the mirror was cracked into a million pieces. They'd replaced all the mirrors yesterday, and Eve had immediately smashed them again.

"I'm ready. Hang on." Persephone let the door swing shut, then emerged again a few seconds later.

"Why do you shave your head?" I realized how that sounded, and quickly added, "I'm not saying it doesn't look good. It's just a look you don't often see."

Persephone ran her hand over her freshly shaved stubble. "One day, after our school football team had won a big game, one of the players lifted me and carried me around the cafeteria like I was some sort of mascot. Everyone thought it was hilarious. That's when I shaved my head. When you're my size, everyone thinks you're cute. No one takes you seriously. But no one messes with a girl with a shaved head. Not even one who's four foot six."

I ran my hand through my own, more traditional-length hair. "Maybe I should try it. I wouldn't mind being taken more seriously."

Persephone turned, "I'll get my razor."

"*No!* I was only . . ." I took an involuntary step back before I saw her grin, and realized she was only joking. "Very funny."

Lorena stepped out of the dorm room wearing an oversized Arianna Grande concert t-shirt.

"I wouldn't have pegged you for an Arianna fan," Persephone said.

Lorena made a face. "It's a hand-me-down." She fell into step beside us as we headed out.

"What does your prompter sound like?" Persephone asked me.

I shrugged. "I don't know. A man."

"Old?"

"Not that I can tell."

"Mine's old—" Persephone stopped talking just as my earbud guy started.

"Direction. That's enough, Ben. Talk like you're in school at home."

For two weeks, they'd been cutting in to stop us from talking about what was going on, and it was getting old. You couldn't even sneak off and talk in a park, because wherever you were, they could hear you.

When we reached the classroom, I took my seat beside Eve. I was still terrified of her—we all were—but I wasn't *as* terrified. Mostly she just ignored us. And, as my psychologist had explained to me, your body only had so much adrenaline. No matter how terrifying the situation, eventually the anxiety has to subside at least a little.

"How you doing?" Earbud Guy said.

I turned to Eve and cleared my throat. "How you doing?"

Every day my prompter made me try to strike up conversations with Eve, and every day she ignored me.

"You coming to the movie tonight?" he prompted. I repeated the words. Of course Eve was coming to the movie. Eve always came to the movie and sat by herself and hissed at anyone who wandered too close. Eve loved movies, food, and rides. We were pretty sure that was why those things were here in abundance. Everything revolved around Eve. I was sure we were here because of her (not the other way around, as Persephone kept insisting), but I had no idea *why*.

We started class with how to negotiate politely yet firmly. *I appreciate you lowering your asking price on this car to twelve thousand dollars, but, gee, I really can't afford more than ten thousand.* This would come in handy *never*.

Ms. Bazzini stepped down the row in her sensible black shoes. "Come on, Eve, practice this one with me?" Now, this was new. Ms. Bazzini never left the front of the room. "I'll be the seller, you be the buyer. All right?" She squatted by Eve's desk. "I know you can talk. Can't—"

Ms. Bazzini let out a tight, muffled shriek and backed away from Eve, holding her cheek. Droplets of blood squeezed between her fingers and trickled down her hand. Eve was still hardened, barbed, and hissing. I hadn't seen what she'd done—it had been too quick.

When Eve opened her mouth, I almost fell out of my seat. "I can talk. Don't tell me when." Her voice was wet, hissing.

I nearly wet my pants. Ms. Spain strode into the room, looking in charge. A nurse in a white uniform was on her heels. The nurse whisked Ms. Bazzini away. She left a trail of blood droplets, starting a few feet from my desk and trailing out the classroom door.

I expected Ms. Spain to say something about what had just happened—I think everyone did—but she just picked up where Ms. Bazzini had left off. Except she didn't even look in Eve's direction.

I didn't look in Eve's direction either. Instead, I exchanged a look with Persephone, then Lorena. Enough was enough. If my mom and dad knew what was happening here—if they knew that one of my classmates was a dangerous, psychotic *creature*—they'd be pounding on that gate. All of the parents would.

At least, I *thought* they would. Was it possible my mother, at least, knew this school was dangerous, and had sent me anyway? I mean, she was CIA. Wouldn't she of all people have to know what was going on in here?

Either way, I wanted out. This was insane. Why weren't we all running for the door to get as far away from Eve as we could before she went completely nuts and started lashing out at all of us? Why weren't security people racing in here to take Eve away? After seeing what she'd done to Ms. Bazzini, how *fast* she'd done it, I had no doubt she could kill us all if she decided to.

We sat obediently as Ms. Spain taught us the polite way to negotiate a deal. I wasn't paying attention, though; I was planning my escape.

CHAPTER 8

"Still think she's a hoax?" Lorena asked Persephone as tall grass and weeds tugged at our legs. We'd decided to take a walk around the perimeter. Our earbud guys didn't say anything, so we figured it was okay.

"I don't know. Maybe."

Lorena threw her hands in the air. "How can you *say* that? You were there. You saw what happened." I expected Earbud Guy to cut in and tell us to change the subject any second. Except they sometimes let us talk if we were someplace where no one could possibly overhear.

"It was exactly what you'd do if you wanted to convince someone Eve was real. Did you actually see the wound? All we saw was Ms. Bazzini holding her face, and blood. It could have been fake blood."

"What about the way Ms. Bazzini *reacted?*" I said. "No one could fake that."

Persephone made a *get a clue* face at me. "You ever seen a movie?"

I sighed heavily, exasperated. I got that Persephone was a skeptic, but after what had just happened, I couldn't believe she still thought this was all being staged.

"No dude in a costume can move that fast. Nothing can." Lorena paused, then added, "Nothing from *this* world, anyway."

Persephone let out an impatient sigh. "Now we're back to demons."

Lorena stopped walking. She was glaring at Persephone. "You know what I think? I think you're afraid to admit it's not a guy in a suit, because if you do, your whole skeptical, logical world comes tumbling down around you, and that scares you more than anything."

Persephone folded her arms. "You don't know anything about me."

Lorena smiled. "I know more than you might think."

"Let me guess: because you can sense my *qi?*" Persephone's voice dripped sarcasm.

"Exactly."

"The point *is*," I cut in, "whatever Eve is, she's not a hoax. She's *dangerous.*" Arguments made my stomach clench, even if I wasn't the one arguing.

A flash of movement in the woods beyond the fence caught my eye. I stopped walking. "Look at that." A soldier in camo fatigues, carrying a rifle, disappeared back into the foliage.

Lorena looked at Persephone. "This is an amazingly elaborate hoax. An actor who can move as fast as The Flash. Soldiers with rifles patrolling the perimeter. Those rifles are probably just props that shoot blanks."

Persephone wiped a droplet of sweat from the side of her bald head. "Okay. You've made your point."

I took that as Persephone's stubborn way of admitting Eve wasn't a guy in a suit and started to say that we had to get out of this place before Eve killed us all. Then I remembered the earbud. Even out here, they were listening.

As I tried to think of a way we could talk without being overheard, the distant roar of The Cyclone coaster caught my attention. The carnival was running.

"Come on, let's take a ride on The Cyclone." I raised my eyebrows, silently signaling to Lorena and Persephone that I had something up my sleeve.

CHAPTER 9

Persephone leaned into me as we rattled around a sharp curve on The Cyclone. I shifted closer to the door, a handle digging into my hip. There wasn't much room in our little car.

Lorena showed us a slip of paper. *Stow away in the back of the food truck?*

I shook my head, then jotted, *They watch us every minute.*

Persephone nodded as she read what I'd written.

We couldn't climb over that huge fence in the middle of the night or stow away in the back of the truck that delivered fresh food every day. This wasn't *Mission: Impossible*. We needed something realistic.

The train of coaster cars began its slow climb to the corkscrew plunge that gave The Cyclone its name. If there was one place they didn't have cameras watching us, it was here. We were moving too fast.

Persephone passed us a slip of paper. *Pretend we're sick?*

Stomach pain, like we all had food poisoning or a virus? Only you almost always threw up when you had something contagious like that. It wasn't like we'd all come down with appendicitis at the same time. For all we knew, the school had its own hospital, and we'd find ourselves undergoing invasive tests right here in Sagantown.

When I shook my head, Persephone nodded immediately, like she'd already come to the same conclusion.

We reached the top of the hill. I felt that weightless, butterfly feeling in my stomach as we plunged almost straight down, then hit the corkscrew and spun. I gripped the metal safety bar with both hands. Some of the kids in front of us had their hands in the air.

"*Wait*—" Lorena's words got whipped away by the wind, drowned out by the roar of the roller coaster. I waited, jaw clenched, for The Cyclone to flatten out.

The train of cars slowed and jerked to a stop as we pulled into the station. We hopped out.

"Once more." Lorena raised my eyebrows to signal

that we needed a little more private time. It would be our sixth consecutive ride on The Cyclone, and my stomach was already queasy, but Lorena looked as if she was dying to share an idea.

As we jerked out of the station and headed toward the first hill, Lorena wrote frantically, then passed what she'd written to Persephone, who read it and passed it along to me.

The only way to get out of here is to stop being the sort of kids that made them choose us in the first place. She had underlined "first." I gave her a questioning look.

Lorena took back the paper, wrote something beneath what she'd already written, and passed it back.

Be bad. Stop obeying.

My eyes went wide, and my stomach clenched. I was not a rebel. I'd never been sent to the principal's office in my entire life.

I looked at Persephone, who seemed intrigued.

I was pretty sure I wouldn't be able to misbehave with everyone looking at me and Earbud Guy shouting orders in my ear. I'd try, but obedience was so engrained in me. I just couldn't be the bad kid. Lorena, on the other hand, seemed like a natural with her quick wit, and Persephone was a protestor. She was all about civil disobedience for a right cause, and saving our skins was a right cause. Maybe I could sit this one out and egg them on from the sidelines.

CHAPTER 10

"Lorena, what's with you today?" Ms. Spain asked. Everyone was staring at Lorena and at the notebook pages she'd just flung into the air.

"I don't know what to tell you, Ms. Spain. I'm in a terrible mood. Everything is annoying me. Including you."

"Why don't you grow up?" Grace said under her breath.

"I know, right?" Bella Jenkins added.

Ms. Spain just shook her head. "Let's get back on track. I'd like each of you to take a look at the countries highlighted on the maps I gave you and predict what their number one natural resource is."

"Can you help me with this?" the guy in my ear instructed me to say. "I'm not sure I understand what she wants."

He wanted me to ask Eve for help with something? That was awfully close to what Ms. Bazzini had been doing when Eve ripped her face. There didn't seem to be any limit to the danger they were willing to put us in. I was tempted to ask him why he didn't come out of whatever safe little room he was hiding in and ask Eve himself.

Be bad. Stop obeying.

This was my chance to do my part, I realized. I didn't have to make a scene, I just needed to ignore Earbud Guy.

With my heart pounding so hard I could hear the blood rushing behind my ears, I continued working on the stupid assignment.

"Do not repeat. Are you all right? Scratch your nose if you are, scratch your wrist if you're not," The prompter said in my ear.

I did neither. I wanted to, but I didn't.

"Do not repeat. Ben, I know you're scared, but believe me, we know what we're doing. Now, turn toward Eve."

Had Ms. Bazzini *not* known what she was doing? I guess no one had bothered to give her an earbud so she could have an all-knowing, infallible voice tell her not to enrage the monster in the room.

"Direction. Turn toward Eve," the all-knowing, infallible voice repeated. "Ask her if she wants to ride The Cyclone with you, Persephone, and Lorena tonight."

My palms were so slick, it was hard to grip my pencil, but I did nothing.

"Do not repeat. Ben, please, don't let me down. Don't let *us* down. This is more important than you know."

"*No*," I said out loud, startling myself. Everyone looked my way; Ms. Spain stopped talking. "I'm not saying it." I was so scared I thought I might vomit. I'd never, ever talked that way to an adult.

"Excuse me, I have to go to the bathroom." Earbud Guy sounded angry. "Say it, then get up and get out of that room."

I looked at Lorena, who mouthed, *You are awesome.* Then Persephone, who nodded, her eyes blazing.

I took the earbud out of my ear and dropped it on the floor.

Everyone gaped at me. Except Ms. Spain, who actually looked scared.

Then I realized why she looked scared.

Eve was looking at me.

I glanced at Eve, then away.

"I like you," Eve said.

The words terrified me more than if Eve had said she hated me. I didn't know what to do. Everyone was staring at me, gape-mouthed. I had to answer. If I ignored her, it might make her mad.

So breathless I could barely get the words out, I said, "Thanks. I like you too." I wanted to run. I so wanted to run.

Ms. Spain turned to the board and went on with her lesson, her voice shaking.

Eve went on looking at me. I could see her in my peripheral vision, her tiny, sunken eyes, circled by what looked like ears, fixed on me.

How much longer did I have to sit here? I checked the old-fashioned clock on the wall. Almost an hour. An hour to sit here sweating and shaking. Would Eve go on looking at me that whole time? I had a feeling she would.

CHAPTER 11

"Benjamin," Ms. Spain said. She and a white-haired man with a goatee, dressed in a brown suit, were waiting outside the classroom. Ms. Spain gestured for me to go with them. My knees still shaking, I followed them out a side door, across the quad.

The two adults didn't speak as we walked. Were they going to kick me out of the school and send me home? I hoped so. Lorena and Persephone could use the same strategy to make their own escapes.

We passed the cafeteria to a squat, white building by the access road. Inside, the hallway was so new you could smell fresh paint and sawdust. We turned into a nice office with wood trim, where a short, bull-necked man with a gray crewcut sprang up and came around his desk, his hand out.

"Hello, Benjamin. I'm Randall Winn, the principal here at Sagan Middle." It felt weird to shake the principal's hand with my sweaty one. Principals didn't shake students' hands or give their first names. Winn gestured at the old guy with the goatee. "This is Mr. Pierre, and you already know Ms. Spain, our vice-principal."

They both nodded to me.

"That was quite a meltdown you had in there," Principal Winn said, his tone conversational, almost as if he was admiring how impressively I'd melted down.

They were all looking at me. They didn't look angry, more like concerned. Still, I felt put on the spot as they waited for some sort of reply from me.

"Sorry about that," I finally muttered.

"Can you tell us what brought it on?" Mr. Pierre asked. Either he had a very slight accent, or just an odd way of pronouncing words.

"I just don't think I'm right for this school," I said. "I have an anxiety disorder."

They exchanged looks, like they were trying to decide who should answer.

"Yes, we're aware of that, Benjamin," Ms. Spain said.

"Well, this place is making it much worse, and I'd like to go home, please." Why hadn't I thought of this earlier? Just tell them I want to go home.

"I'm afraid that's not possible." Principal Winn sounded sorry. Sad, even.

"Just call my mother. She'll come and get me." At least, I hoped she would.

Winn shook his head. "I'm afraid no one can leave until the semester is done."

It felt as if the walls of the room had suddenly closed in on all sides, making the room feel much smaller. "You can't *force* us to stay here."

Winn set a sheet of paper onto the desk. "Your mother agreed to very specific terms, and she is your legal guardian. That's her signature, isn't it?" He pushed the paper closer.

I looked at the paper. "She doesn't know what's going on in here."

"Yes, she does, Benjamin." Ms. Spain spoke softly, like she was talking to a young child.

I pointed in the direction of the school. "Did you see what happened to Ms. Bazzini?"

"Ms. Bazzini is fine," Ms. Spain said.

"Well that's funny, because nobody's seen her. And what about the next person who gets Eve angry? How do you know they'll be okay? She *likes* me now."

"Don't worry about Eve, Benjamin. We have her under control," Principal Winn said.

Under control? She didn't seem under control to me.

"What *is* she?" I asked.

No one answered.

Ms. Spain turned in her seat. "Benjamin, we can't tell you much, but believe me when I say it's *very* important that you help us. You made a breakthrough in there just now, even if it wasn't according to plan." She reached over and patted my knee. "Please. Be the boy we know you are."

"And please keep this in your ear." Principal Winn set a fresh earbud still in its cellophane wrapper on the desk in front of me.

"I don't know. I think he should leave it out." Mr. Pierre was small and thin, his nose oddly shaped so you could see partway into his nostrils. "Eve likes him because he tossed the earbud away. I think we should run with that, maybe even instruct some of his classmates to toss away theirs in the same show of defiance."

Principal Winn raised his eyebrows and tilted his head as if maybe he'd heard Mr. Pierre wrong. "You want to leave what to say up to this twelve-year-old boy?"

Mr. Pierre spread his hands. "He's the one who made the breakthrough."

Principal Winn exhaled loudly through his nose. He waved at Pierre. "Okay. We'll give it a try for now."

Mr. Pierre turned to me. "Try to bring Eve out of her shell. Encourage her to get to know your friends. Show her what it's like to be a twelve-year-old."

"I'm thirteen," I said.

"I apologize," Mr. Pierre said. "A thirteen-year-old."

I considered. "*Why* can't you tell me what she is?"

"We can't tell you that," the principal replied.

"You can't tell me why you can't tell me?"

He nodded. "That's right."

I wanted to go home. I wanted to go home and binge-watch *Annoying Orange*. Except Mom wanted me *here*, and if Ms. Spain was telling the truth, Mom knew exactly what that meant.

Mr. Pierre patted me on the back awkwardly, as if he wasn't used to interacting with kids. "Go work your magic. Bring Eve out of her shell. We're counting on you."

I could tell they wanted me to say something like, *I'll do my best*, or *I won't let you down*, but I left without saying a word. I didn't want to have anything to do with Eve. I wanted to stay as far away from her as I could.

CHAPTER 12

The movie that night was *Star Wars* Episode X: *Battle of the Jedi*, which wasn't going to be released in theaters for another month. These people had pull, that was for sure. I took my usual seat in the back row of the small theater with Lorena and Persephone.

"'Show her what it's like to be a twelve-year-old?' That's what he said?" Lorena asked.

"Yep," I said.

Persephone made a disgusted noise. "They don't even know how old we are."

"Why would they want to do that?" Lorena asked. "It's like they're studying her, trying to learn more about her."

"Or us," Persephone suggested.

Drew, who was sitting a row in front of us, turned around. "Has anyone seen Ms. Bazzini?"

"No," Lorena said. "She just sort of vanished."

"I've been thinking about it all day," Drew said. "What if Ms. Bazzini wasn't *cut*, she was *stung*? And what if Eve's stings are poisonous?"

Things suddenly got really quiet. That had never even occurred to me. Since we didn't know what Eve *was*, we had no idea what she was capable of.

Grace, who was sitting in the row in front of Drew, spun around and gave Drew an exasperated huff. "They wouldn't put a bunch of seventh graders in with someone who was *poisonous*."

"Of course not," Lorena said. "They'd only put us in with someone who cuts your face if you make her angry." I gave Lorena a warning nudge, as Eve appeared from out of the breezeway. Instead of heading to her usual spot in the front, she paused.

She began climbing the steps.

"Oh no," I moaned through clenched teeth.

Eve kept climbing, head down, until she reached our row. She lumbered over to us, took the two seats beside me, and, munching popcorn from a plastic tub, looked me over.

Why had I tossed my earbud away? Suddenly I wanted an adult telling me what to say, because I had no idea. I kept flashing to Ms. Bazzini clutching her face, the blood dribbling down her arm.

I swallowed. This was getting weird with Eve staring at me, everyone else watching while pretending they weren't, the entire theater deadly quiet.

I gazed up into Eve's enormous face—her wide, lipless mouth, eyes that were nothing but holes surrounded by a circular earlobe, a wide, flat nose. "Have you seen any of the other *Star Wars* movies?" My voice was an octave higher than usual.

"No." Her voice was hissing and watery.

"They're really good." My mouth was so dry my upper lip was sticking to my front teeth as I spoke, and my knees were shaking uncontrollably. "When you get a chance, you should definitely see them."

"They think I'm stupid."

A jolt of electric panic ran right down to my toes. I wanted to stick to small talk, watch the movie, then race to my bed and hide under the blankets for a week. I felt like I was on much thinner ice, talking about serious things with her. If I said the wrong thing, she might get angry. I had to say something, though. She was looking at me. Waiting.

"The people talking to us in our earbuds, you mean?"

"All of them."

I nodded. I didn't know where to go from there. I gave Lorena and Persephone a look—*Help me out here.*

They just went on staring. Why weren't their prompters feeding them lines? I was dying here. One wrong word and I would end up like Ms. Bazzini.

"Do you know why I'm here?" Eve asked.

The question startled me. "You don't know either?"

"No."

"No one tells us anything. We all thought *you* knew." I looked to my friends and raised my eyebrows, begging for some help here.

Persephone leaned forward, snapping herself out of her stupor. "Where were you before this?"

"Another school," Eve said. "Alone with the teachers. Before that, the lab. Machines. Tests. No windows. There were four of us."

"What about before that?" I didn't want to come right out and ask, *What are you?*

"That's all. The lab, then the school."

I'd convinced myself Eve was an alien who'd crashed in a UFO and was taken to Area 51. But if she'd crashed in a UFO, she'd remember that. Evidently I was wrong. And if she was a guy in a costume, he deserved an Oscar. If he was a guy in a costume, I'd eat my dirty laundry.

A wave of relief washed over me as the lights dimmed. The movie was starting. We all turned to watch.

Eve went through her tub of popcorn in five minutes. She raised the empty tub. A guy in a red theater uniform ran to get her more.

My armpits were slick with sweat, my bowels twisting with fear. I had to admit, though: I was also a little excited. People kept glancing back to look at us, wide-eyed, awestruck that I was actually sitting beside Eve, even talking to her. It was like walking along the ledge of a tall building or diving off a cliff into water of unknown depth.

Lorena raised her empty bucket in the air. The guy in red raised a finger and ran to get her more.

"Nice," Lorena said, laughing. Usually the rest of us had to get our own at the concession stand.

CHAPTER 13

As the credits rolled, Eve lumbered toward the exit without a word. Everyone else stayed in their seats, afraid to get too close to her. My neck and shoulder muscles relaxed; I'd been clenching them for the past two-plus hours without realizing it.

"Well that was . . . interesting," Persephone said as we made our way down the steps.

I wiped my palms on my shirt. "I was so afraid I was going to say something that made her mad." I couldn't quite get Drew's idea that Eve might be poisonous out of my head.

"Now that we've talked to her, I feel kind of sad for her," Lorena said. "When she asked if we knew why she was here? She sounded so lost."

"I'd feel more sorry for her if she hadn't done what she did to Ms. Bazzini," I said.

"I thought you said she was a demon," Persephone said.

"I said she's not of this world," Lorena said. "That doesn't necessarily mean she's evil."

We exited the theater into the chilly fall evening. "What do you want to do now?" I asked.

"How about some ice cream?" Persephone suggested.

We headed toward the ice cream shop.

Eve was standing a ways down from the theater, her strange, short, boneless arms dangling at her sides. She did that a lot—just stood there, not looking around, not doing anything.

"We should ask her to join us," Lorena said.

I chuckled dryly. "I dare you."

Lorena stopped walking. "She's all alone. She doesn't have parents, or friends, or a real home. No one deserves to be that alone, even someone as mean as Eve. It's probably the *reason* she's so mean."

I hadn't thought of it that way, but now that Lorena had laid it out, it rang so true. I still didn't relish the idea of eating ice cream with someone who could get angry at any little thing and could *hurt* you. Seriously *hurt* you. Maybe even kill you.

"I'm going to." Lorena turned and called, "Eve, do

you want to get ice cream with us?"

Eve just went on standing there, arms dangling.

"Well, you tried," Persephone said. We continued on toward the ice cream shop.

Persephone glanced back. "*Look.*"

Eve was following us.

"*Whoa,*" Lorena said.

Persephone held the door for Lorena and me, then kept holding it for Eve.

As the four of us entered, the conversation inside stopped. My palms and armpits were sweating like mad, but suddenly we were friends with a terrifying creature, and that was weirdly cool.

"What's your favorite flavor?" I asked Eve as we stepped up to the counter.

"It all tastes the same," Eve said. "But it's a good taste."

As soon as the guy working the counter, who had amazingly good posture and hair that looked as if it had been cut that morning, saw Eve, he spun and made her a ridiculously large sundae. Eve didn't have to say a word.

We picked an empty table as the other kids snuck glances our way.

An awkward silence stretched. I had no idea what to say to someone who'd grown up in a lab.

"So Eve, what was it like for you as a kid?" Lorena asked. "Did you have toys?"

"No toys. Injections."

I swallowed. What do you say to that?

Lorena covered her mouth, her eyes filling with tears. "You poor thing. That sounds *awful.*"

Eve stared at Lorena. She looked . . . surprised, maybe?

"What happened to the other three . . . people in the lab?" Persephone asked.

Eve studied Persephone with her scary-looking ear-eyes. "Did they tell you to ask that?" There was a not-so-subtle threat in her hissing, warbling voice.

"*No,*" Persephone said quickly. "I was just wondering."

I nudged Persephone's elbow. "Ditch your earbud. What are they going to do? Nothing happened to *me.*" It felt kind of good to be the bad boy. I'd never been the bad boy before. It was also a little terrifying.

"That's true. Why am I still wearing this thing?" Persephone took the earbud out and went to put it in her pocket.

I grasped her hand. "No. Chuck it."

Persephone smiled at me, then chucked the earbud with all of her might. It bounced off the storefront window. A few of the onlookers gasped. One girl laughed.

Persephone looked at Lorena and raised her eyebrows. "Your turn."

Lorena had already taken hers out and was tossing it up and down in her palm. She whipped it at Grace.

"Incoming!"

"Jerk," Grace hissed.

Eve seemed satisfied. She turned to Persephone. "One disappeared a few years ago. Two were bad. Mean. They were kept separate from us. I almost never saw them."

They were *mean*? If Eve was the nice one, I didn't want to meet the mean ones. Were they genetic experiments? If they were, that led to the same question as every other possible explanation: Why would they be putting on this whole middle school thing for a genetic experiment? To learn more about Eve? Was this all some sort of experiment?

Eve leaned in toward the center of the table and lowered her voice. "Do you know what I *am*?" Even with her strange voice, it was impossible to miss the pain in her words.

"We don't," I said. "*They* must know, though. When they pulled me into the office, I asked, but they wouldn't say."

At the table next to ours, Lucian and Grace took out their earbuds and set them on the table. *All* of the kids were taking them out.

"What's going on?" I asked Grace, who looked like she'd gotten even less sleep in the past two weeks than I had.

"The prompters told us to take them out."

"Good," Lorena said. "Now they can't tell anyone

what we can and can't talk about."

"They're still listening." Persephone looked up toward the ceiling. "You know they are."

Lorena shrugged. "Let them listen."

There was an awkward silence, because Eve was right there, so we couldn't talk about her, and most of the kids were too scared to talk directly *to* her.

Lorena finally broke the silence. "With all of the buildings on this campus, you'd think they could have given us our own rooms."

"I know, right?" a tall girl a few tables away said. "And the classes here are *lame*. I thought this was supposed to be an accelerated curriculum."

"Does anyone know what this place really is or why we're here?" Persephone asked, cutting through the tiptoeing around.

"They told us what it is before we came." Grace said. "It's an elite program. A pilot program that could go nationwide."

Persephone made a sound in the back of her throat. "An elite program where all the kids wear earbuds and are told what to say. Right."

"Why are you all so negative?" Lucian asked. "Why can't you just trust the people in charge and follow the rules?"

Persephone pressed her index finger to her chin. "Um, because the people in charge aren't trustworthy?"

Lucian shook his head in disgust. "You're going to ruin this for all of us."

"Ruin what?" I asked.

Lucian leaned toward me. He kept side-glancing at Eve, as if she might leap at him at any second. "My father told me if I completed this program successfully, my future would be so bright, I'd have to squint."

Persephone shook her head and muttered, "More bribes." She turned to face Grace. "Did you ever stop to wonder *why* they're saying all these great things are going to happen if we complete the program?"

"Because it's an elite program, and we'll be part of the inaugural class." Grace gave Persephone a look, and added, "Duh."

I was watching Eve out of the corner of my eye. It was an elite program designed for the best and brightest, where we were taught bizarre subjects that weren't particularly challenging, except to one very large, very strange-looking student. "Did you know we're not allowed to leave? You can't drop out and go home, for any reason."

From the looks on their faces, they hadn't known that.

"We have a right to know what's going on," Persephone said. "So does Eve."

Grace put her hands on her narrow hips. "Why don't you tell them that?"

"Maybe I will."

Grace rolled her eyes. "You're *thirteen*. They must have a good reason for not telling us everything that's going on, or they'd tell us." I'd seen Grace take her earbud out, but she talked like she was still being fed lines by one of the adult monitors.

"There are soldiers with automatic rifles patrolling the woods." Lucian wiped a spot of chocolate ice cream off the side of his mouth. "This is serious government stuff. They know what they're doing. Don't mess things up."

"Things are already messed up," Eve hissed. Her body got a little sharper, a little harder.

Lucian shrank into his chair. Three kids sitting near the door hurried out. The rest sat stock still, doing their best impersonations of store mannequins.

"I don't want to go back to the lab," Eve continued. "Adam isn't there anymore, and they won't tell me where they took him. When we were good, they used to let us watch TV. Adam liked *Teen Titans*. He got most of the surgery."

You could almost hear the ice cream melting, it was so quiet.

The door swung open. Jacob poked his head inside. When he spotted Eve sitting with us, his eyes went wide. I thought he was going to duck right back out, but instead he swallowed, his big Adam's apple bobbing, and said, "They shut the phone off."

"*What?*" about four of us said more or less in unison.

"Why?" Grace asked.

"My prompter says it's because people aren't following the rules," Jacob said.

Lucian glared at Persephone, then at me. "See? This is all your fault."

"Your prompters haven't said anything about it?" Jacob asked.

I glanced at Lorena's earbud lying on the tile near Jacob's foot.

"No," Grace answered.

"Well, we're not allowed to call home anymore." Jacob shut the door and took off, probably off to tell others.

"They're treating us like prisoners," Persephone said. "We're surrounded by fences, our conversations are being monitored, there are guards. Now we can't even talk to our parents?"

"We should do something," I said.

"But *what?*" Lorena didn't say it, but it was in the tone of her voice: *We're thirteen. What can we do?*

We could continue with the original plan. We could be bad. They'd handpicked a bunch of kids who would obey their rules. We could stop being those kids.

"Haven't you three already done enough?" Lucian asked. I think he wanted to say more, but he kept glancing at Eve. I think he was afraid if he got on us too hard, it might make Eve angry.

"We should organize a protest," Persephone said, ignoring Lucian.

"Yes, why don't you carry signs in front of that town hall building?" Grace said, rolling her eyes. "I'm sure that will help."

Lorena inhaled sharply. "I know what we should do."

I leaned closer. "Tell us."

Grinning, Lorena jumped out of her seat, picked up her sundae, and threw it. The ice cream made a wet *splat* on the black and white tile. She raised her fist in the air and screamed, "We're not going to take it!"

"Yes!" I shouted as vanilla ice cream and strawberry sauce splattered.

Persephone leaped to her feet. "Strike! No more bribes. We want rights!" She grabbed her banana split and flung it at the floor.

Eve was watching all of this carefully. She looked at me, at my sundae, and back at me. She seemed curious to see what I would do.

I wasn't sure what I should do. I wanted to back up my friends, and I agreed with the reasons for the protest, but I was also scared. I was a "stand on the periphery and cheer you on" sort of guy, not an action guy.

My heart racing, I swept my chocolate fudge sundae off the table. The bowl clattered across the black and white linoleum floor, spewing melted ice cream and fudge sauce. I burst out laughing, liking the way it felt.

"Oh, that's really mature," Grace said.

Grace, Lucian, and most of the other kids headed toward the door, probably afraid they'd get in trouble. Three brave souls stayed behind with us, hurling their own sundaes.

Eve watched, her hands dangling at her sides. *Show her what it's like to be a twelve-year-old kid*, the principal had said. *This* was what it was like. What it should be like, anyway. Being crazy, making a mess, laughing till your stomach hurt. Only, until now, *we* hadn't really known what it was like, because we were the good kids, working our butts off with an eye toward college. Playing on the soccer team even if we didn't like it, filling every free minute with homework and extracurricular activities.

I vaulted the counter, where tubs in thirty flavors waited. I figured I'd have to duck around the server, but he just stood and watched, arms crossed, as I dug out a snowball-sized dollop of peanut butter fudge ripple with my bare hand and threw it at Persephone, nailing her in the back.

Laughing, Persephone scooped a handful of her sundae off the floor and whipped it at me. I ducked, avoiding most of it. I wiped the rest from my cheek with the back of my sleeve and noticed that we now had an audience. A dozen or more of our classmates were standing outside, watching the carnage through the windows.

I froze with my hand in the rocky road as loud hissing cut through the air like a busted steam pipe.

Eve was standing, dwarfing the rest of us, her dish in her hand. Spines had popped out all over her, tearing holes in her dress. She hurled the sundae at the wall so hard the bowl shattered.

I raised a clenched fist in the air as Lorena and Persephone let out a ragged cheer.

Eve stalked behind the counter, pulled an entire tub of black raspberry, and hurled it at the wall. The cardboard tub split, spraying purple ice cream in all directions.

Lorena retrieved a double handful of black raspberry from the floor and dumped it over another girl's head. The girl squealed with laughter and went to get some to retaliate with.

I kicked the remnants of a tub lying on the floor. Fudge ripple ice cream splattered all over my shoe and pant leg.

Eve grabbed tub after tub, jettisoning them across the shop. She was fully barbed, her skin reflecting the light like polished stone. She wasn't laughing—she was enraged.

The others had mostly stopped to watching Eve. Lorena pumped her fists, egging Eve on as Persephone smiled uneasily, and the other kids gawked, wide-eyed.

When Eve was finished with the tubs, she went after the machinery, smashing it flat with hard fists, then swept glasses, steel milkshake shakers, and boxes of napkins off the shelves. It was like she had an on-off switch and it had been switched to *on*. I had a feeling if someone accidentally got in her way, they'd get hurt.

Eve stood in the middle of the ice cream shop, looking left and right for something else to wreck. There was nothing—she'd demolished the place.

Hissing like a steam engine, she charged out of the shop and into the night.

Lorena looked at me, elated, her breath coming in gasps. "Where's she going?"

I shrugged. "No idea."

We took off after her. The small crowd gathered outside gaped as we passed, then followed at a safe distance. Part of me wanted to hang back, to slow down and join the cautious kids, but I kept going.

Eve galloped across the quad, making a beeline for our school. She stormed right up and hit the double front doors like a linebacker. They didn't budge.

Hissing furiously, Eve yanked on a door handle, tearing it right off. She flung it aside and charged right at the still-closed doors. This time they burst open.

She disappeared into the darkness beyond.

"Come on." Persephone took off after her. We followed Persephone into the main hallway. It wasn't hard to follow the booms and crashes Eve was making deeper inside the school.

We watched from the doorway of our classroom as Eve lifted a desk over her head and hurled it through the window, out onto the lawn. This was terrifying. She was going way beyond being a typical thirteen-year-old, but it felt wrong to back out of the protest because Eve had kicked it up a notch. It scared me, but it also felt right.

I stepped past Persephone and joined Eve in what was left of the classroom.

I ripped the world map off the wall and tore it to pieces. I didn't have anything against maps; I found them interesting, actually. But it felt satisfying to rip it apart.

I ducked as a chair flew uncomfortably close to my head, while simultaneously straining to tip the teacher's desk. The big desk suddenly got lighter. I looked up to find Lorena helping me. Books and papers sprayed off it, scattering across the floor.

I was shaking all over, a mix of terror and rage. I felt sure I was going to end up in jail for this, or that when there was nothing left to smash, Eve would turn on us and smash us too. But it also felt good.

There wasn't an adult in sight. The soldiers in the woods stayed where they were while Eve threw desks through windows.

When there was nothing left to destroy, we headed into the hallway. Some of our fellow students were scrawling graffiti on the walls with markers. Bangs and crashes echoed from rooms down the hall. If we were going to get in trouble for this, at least we weren't the only ones.

Eve stepped in front of us. I expected her to go barreling down the hallway, but instead, she just stood there.

Slowly, steadily, the barbs covering her shrank, until her plum-colored skin was once again smooth.

"I'm tired," Eve said. She trudged off down the hallway.

Trailing a few paces behind, we followed her. I wasn't sure if we'd accomplished anything, or what sort of trouble we were in, and right then, I didn't care. I was tired too. If we were in trouble, we were *all* in trouble, Eve included.

CHAPTER 14

I was dragged out of a nightmare by the sound of someone screaming.

"*Daddy! I want my dad. I want my dad.*" It was Drew. I could see his silhouette in the darkness, scrabbling out of bed. He crawled on hands and knees until he reached the corner closest to Lorena and me and curled up into a ball.

Lorena hopped out of her bed and went to sit beside him. "It's okay. You had a nightmare."

"I want to go home. I want to go home and sleep in my own bed."

Ms. Spain appeared in the doorway. She hurried over to Drew and squatted down. "What's the matter?" she whispered.

"I want to go home right now," Drew wailed.

"Shh. It's okay."

"No, it isn't. Don't let her get me."

From across the room, Eve hissed.

Drew squealed and tried to press himself even further into the corner. "She climbed in my bed while I was sleeping. I woke up, and she was *right there*."

"Liar!" Eve cried. "You liar!"

"It was just a nightmare," Ms. Spain said.

I winced at Ms. Spain's choice of words. Eve made a ton of noise getting in and out of her cot, so no doubt Ms. Spain was right that Drew had just dreamed it. But if we were trying to make Eve feel like one of the gang, calling a dream where Eve climbs in bed with you "a nightmare" didn't advance the cause.

"No, it wasn't," Drew wailed. "I want to go home!"

"Come on." Ms. Spain helped Drew to his feet and led him toward the door.

As they drew close to her, Eve hissed angrily, causing Drew to let out another earsplitting screech. Ms. Spain pretty much dragged him past Eve and out the door.

Persephone sighed. "Just another night in Sagantown."

Except it wasn't just another night, I realized. As I eyed the hulking silhouette of Eve in her cot, I had to admit, I still felt scared of her. I could never forget what she'd done to Ms. Bazzini. On top of that, she just *looked* so terrifying. But I also knew she wasn't just some monster out of a nightmare.

Chapter 15

Persephone, Lorena, and I ate our breakfasts in silence, eavesdropping on the conversation at the next table.

"I clogged all the toilets in the bathroom with paper towels and then flushed them," Jacob Warnock said, laughing.

"Jill Sanders climbed on a desk and pulled out a bunch of ceiling tiles, then we broke them over each other's heads," Angela Kang said, giggling.

Half of the kids in the school were talking about the things they'd wrecked, and the other half were grumbling about the kids who had wrecked things. We might as well be wearing shirts to indicate whether we were on Team Protest or Team Rule-Followers.

Everyone was split into camps now. There were the rule followers, led by Grace and Lucian, who were still convinced the adults knew what they were doing and must be obeyed without question. To them, we were dangerous delinquents likely to get them all killed, or at least ruin their chances of getting into a good college. Then there were the kids who agreed with us that this was a messed-up situation, but who were still afraid to get too close to Eve. And then there was us. Actually, you could add a fourth contingent to the mix: kids like Drew, who were paralyzed by their fear and had no opinion beyond wanting to go home. Come to think of it, it was amazing I wasn't in that group. That had always been my group before.

Persephone took a bite of her oatmeal with blueberries, then waved her spoon at us. "You know, last night wasn't just about our parents putting us in a school with a mysterious and potentially violent creature. It was bigger than that. So much of our lives are taken up by worksheets and studying for the next big test. It's boring and stressful, and even when there are no high fences and no Eve, it's a sort of prison."

"I don't know. It's not *that* bad." I didn't love school, but I also didn't think of it as a prison.

"Then why are there *so many* songs about hating school?" Persephone broke into a surprisingly accomplished rendition of the Pink Floyd classic "We

Don't Need No Education," or whatever the song was called. People from nearby tables joined in, laughing. "Why is it there are no songs about hating dentists or acne?" she continued when she'd finished. "Only school."

Lorena and I waited. By now we knew Persephone preferred to answer most of her questions herself.

"Somewhere along the way, adults decided learning shouldn't be fun, that if learning isn't misery, it isn't really learning. I'm interested in a lot of stuff: Politics, computer technology, film theory. I'd *love* to learn more about those things in school. Instead I'm learning about the American Revolution for the twenty-third freaking time. Teachers don't care what we're interested in, they teach us what they think we *should* be interested in."

I could quibble with that. Teachers didn't get to decide what to teach—it was the higher-ups who decided—but I couldn't argue with Persephone's bigger point. Even if I'd wanted to argue, I was learning Persephone was a way better arguer than me, so it was basically pointless to try.

Lorena was looking around the cafeteria. "Where is Eve? She doesn't eat in here anymore."

"Not since she hissed at people and told them not to look at her, no," I said.

"She shouldn't have to eat alone. That's cruel." Lorena stood. "I'm going to see if I can find her and invite her to eat with us."

Persephone stopped chewing. "I'd prefer to eat

without having to worry about being hurled through a window."

"Just because she's different doesn't mean she doesn't deserve love."

Persephone set her spoon down. "I didn't say we should exclude her because she's different. If you started slashing people's faces, I wouldn't want to sit with you either."

"Benjamin." Grace, sitting on the other end of the cafeteria, gestured for me to come over.

"I'll be right back." I headed over to where Grace, Lucian, and a couple of other kids were eating.

As I got closer, I could see Grace was scowling. "They're going to close down the school and send us all home, and we'll all get marks on our permanent records indicating we failed to complete the program. All because of you and your delinquent friends."

"Who told you they're going to close the school?" I asked.

"The principal, that's who." Lucian was so angry he was shaking, his ruddy face even redder than usual.

I glanced back toward my friends, wishing I'd asked them to come with me for moral support.

"Cut it out," Lucian said. "I'm not asking you, I'm telling you."

"Are you threatening me?" I asked.

Lucian scowled. "Just because I'm big doesn't mean

I'm a dumb goon who beats on people who don't do what I say." He stabbed at his temple with his index finger. "Battles are won with your mind, and your mouth, not your fists. That's what Coach says."

Grace stood, hands on hips. "Well, I *am* threatening you. My father is a US senator, and if you screw this up for me, I promise you, my father will make your parents' lives a living hell. They'll be audited every year until they're seventy."

I barked a laugh. "I'd love to see him try to screw with my mom. She's in the CIA."

The room had suddenly grown silent. I looked around, trying to figure out why.

A soldier with a rifle was crossing the cafeteria, coming straight toward us.

Grace followed my gaze. "He's probably here for you. *Good.* I hope they prosecute you and throw you in juvenile detention."

Sure enough, the soldier walked right up to me. "Benjamin?"

"Yes?" I swallowed. I wasn't surprised, but I still had that crawling-terrified sensation in my gut.

"Come with me, please." The soldier turned and headed back across the cafeteria.

With every eye in the place on me, I followed, trailing three paces behind the soldier, feeling incredibly self-conscious.

Halfway across the quad, Persephone caught up to me. "What's going on?"

I shrugged. "He told me to follow him."

Persephone trotted to catch up to the soldier. "Excuse me, but Benjamin didn't cause all that damage on his own. I'm just as responsible as he is."

The soldier kept walking, not even glancing at Persephone.

"*Excuse me,*" Persephone called, louder.

Nothing.

"Oh sure, ignore me. I'm just a kid, after all." She squatted to pull out a handful of grass, then hurled it at the guard. Most of it fluttered to the ground like confetti before reaching him. "There's no need to show me any basic human respect."

I waved Persephone away. "I'll be all right. I'll come find you as soon as I can." If I wasn't locked in a cell or sent home.

Persephone stopped walking. "Are you sure?"

I nodded. "Talk to you later."

I watched the soldier's polished black combat boots rise and fall in the grass, which really needed to be mowed. I wasn't that scared, I realized. My hands were shaking, sure, but it wasn't the icy terror I would have expected, given the situation. Three students watched from the edge of the quad. I lifted my hand, gave them a crisp salute.

Laughing, they saluted back.

I decided to push it a little further. My heart tripping, I cleared my throat and said, "So, do you know what Eve is? I'm not asking you to tell me—I know you can't. I'm just wondering if you know."

The soldier, a stocky African American guy, glanced back, gave me a wry half smile. "Nobody tells me anything."

We passed through Tulipville, where the red, yellow, purple, and white flowers were so bright and perfect they almost looked fake, to the back entrance of the administration building. The soldier held the door for me so that I was leading the way. I headed for Principal Winn's office.

They were all in there waiting for me—Principal Winn sitting behind his desk; Ms. Spain upright in her chair, both feet on the floor; Mr. Pierre, legs crossed, tugging at his goatee.

Winn looked me up and down from behind his desk. "Hello, Benjamin. Have a seat."

I took the empty seat.

Winn heaved a big sigh, tapping a pen on the desk.

"Benjamin, we can't have Eve angry," Mr. Pierre said. "We want her to feel happy."

"How am I supposed to know that?" I asked.

"You're supposed to be wearing an earbud so a qualified adult who *does* know what's going on can guide you, but that cat's out of the bag." Principal Winn dragged a hand through his hair. He looked exhausted, and he'd missed a spot shaving. Not a couple of whiskers, but a big patch on his jaw. "You've got to tone it down. *Way* down."

Staring at that patch of whiskers Winn had missed, it suddenly occurred to me: These people didn't know what they were doing. *Earbuds?* Those had just made Eve angry, and they hadn't anticipated that because *they had no idea what they were doing*. We got Eve better than they did. We got that Eve had a finely tuned lie detector, and when you set it off, she got *pissed*.

"If you let us in on what's happening, maybe we could help," I suggested.

Winn stared at the carpet. "Just, don't make her angry. And stop complaining."

Mr. Pierre put a hand on my shoulder. "You're doing really well, Benjamin. We're grateful to you, and we're astonished by your courage. Just, rein it in. Okay?"

Bring her out of her shell. Rein it in. Trust us. "This is so messed up. There's no special program. You're lying to us. Using us. Is this some sort of experiment? Is that it?"

"It's more complicated than that," Ms. Spain, speaking for the first time, rose from her chair. She squatted right in front of me so we were at eye level. "Please, Benjamin. Please work with us. I promise you, we only have your best interests in mind. You, and the other students. And a lot of others."

I glanced at Principal Winn, who was watching me carefully. Mr. Pierre was leaning forward in his chair. I didn't know how I'd missed it before. They weren't just in over their heads, they were scared.

I rose from my chair and muttered, "I'll do what I can."

"That's all we ask," Mr. Pierre called after me.

"Thank you, Benjamin," Ms. Spain added.

CHAPTER 16

As I headed outside, I turned left instead of right, taking the long way back. I needed time to think.

I couldn't shake the feeling I'd gotten in there, that the adults running this place were terrified and had no idea what they were doing. They were desperate to win Eve over for some reason, but they had no idea how to do it and were just making things up as they went along. Maybe *they* didn't know what Eve was either. Now, *there* was a theory none of us had thought of.

I heard music drifting from somewhere nearby. It was a song by Pink that I couldn't imagine any of the adults here listening to voluntarily. Curious, I headed toward the sound.

It was coming from a tiny, fenced-in courtyard I hadn't noticed before. As I drew close enough to see into it, I stopped short.

Eve was in there. If she hadn't been facing the opposite direction, she would have spotted me immediately. The music was coming from her Harley Davidson's radio, and Eve was moving strangely around the courtyard, shifting from foot to foot, raising and lowering her thin blue arms.

She stopped, then started again, lifting her arms while taking a step forward, then a step back. Was she performing some sort of ritual? Maybe Lorena was right—maybe she was some sort of supernatural creature. She dropped her hands, then moved them stiffly back and forth, almost as if she was trying to . . . floss.

She was trying to dance. It was terrible, truly eye-wateringly terrible, but that was definitely what she was doing.

Eve stopped again. She tried moving just her hands, but it was still awful. She had no rhythm whatsoever.

I backed away slowly and quietly.

There was a sudden *crash*, and the music stopped abruptly. The front end of the motorcycle came flying over the fence, tumbling end-over-end before slamming to the sidewalk twenty feet from me. Eve hissed. The other half of the bike flew into view, as if launched from a catapult. I took off running.

As I slowed to a walk a safe distance from Eve, an image of her jerking back and forth was etched in my mind's eye. She'd seen the kids dancing at that party and was trying to copy them. Trying to be like them. It was so sad, so pathetic, it broke my heart. Suddenly I felt so sorry for her I could hardly stand it.

"*Benjamin.*"

I turned toward the voice. Persephone and Lorena were sitting on a bench in a patch of pink tulips, probably waiting for me.

"What did they say?" Persephone asked as I headed over. "Are they kicking you out?"

I shrugged. "They told me to tone it down."

Persephone's mouth dropped open. "That's it? We did tens of thousands of dollars in damage to their campus, and they told you to *tone it down?*"

I shrugged. "All they care about is Eve. I think they'd happily let us burn this whole place to the ground if it made Eve happy." I pictured Ms. Spain squatting in front of me. "They're scared to death. They won't tell me what it is, but they're scared and desperate, and I don't think they agree on what to do next."

Persephone and Lorena looked at each other.

I remembered the new theory I'd been working on when the Pink song had distracted me. "What if *they* don't know what Eve is? Maybe someone found Eve and the others wandering in the Amazon jungle or something.

That would explain why they were conducting medical experiments on her: they were trying to figure out what she is."

"And they couldn't figure it out, because they're too closed-minded to recognize magical elves when they see them." Persephone looked at Lorena, grinning.

Lorena gave Persephone a gentle shove. "Very funny. Or maybe they haven't thought to look for the zipper in the back of what's obviously a rubber suit."

"Touché." Persephone turned back to me. "The problem with your theory is that if Eve was taken from a rain forest in the Amazon, she'd probably remember."

That was true. "Unless she was really young."

Persephone raised her eyebrows, trying to signal something without the adults overhearing. "Let's take a walk out in the field. I could use some exercise."

She led us out away from the buildings. We pushed through the high grass, leaving our little patch of civilization behind.

"Can they hear us out here if we're not wearing the earbuds?" Lorena asked.

"No," Persephone said.

I looked at Persephone, her sharp, freckled nose and high forehead in profile. "How can you be so sure?"

Persephone pulled a folded sheet from her back pocket. "I mapped the locations of all of their surveillance cameras—"

"*How do you know how to do all of this stuff?*" I interrupted.

"My father's an electrical engineer. He works at the Pentagon. He taught me a bunch of stuff, plus we have a basement full of cutting-edge components and machinery, and I mess around with it and figure it out on my own. Anyway, all of the surveillance cameras are inside and around the buildings. They were counting on the earbuds if we got too far from the campus. That's what I wanted to talk to you about. There are blind spots in their surveillance—routes where you can move around the compound without being seen."

"So?" I asked.

Persephone stopped walking. She stepped close and spoke in a low tone. "So, if no one's going to tell us what's going on, we should find out for ourselves."

Lorena cupped her palm over her mouth. "What an awesome idea. Let's spy on those geezers."

"Wait," I said, "are you suggesting we break into someone's office and go through their files?"

Persephone shrugged. "What's the worst they could do? Suspend us? Kick us out of their elite program?"

It was true, they didn't have many options when it came to punishment. For me, though, the punishment was built in. I would lie awake all night in utter terror if I knew we were going to break into the school administration's computers tomorrow. And actually doing it? I'd probably have a heart attack.

I shook my head. "I can't. It's going way too far."

Lorena grasped my shoulders and pressed her face close to mine. "You know where I really got that Arianna t-shirt? From a donation box at our church. That's where I get all my clothes. My mom works part-time as a secretary at the Department of Education. My father got injured working in a warehouse, and he can't work anymore. Please. I *need* to see for myself that it's not a guy in a suit. I need to know there's magic in the world."

Lorena let her hands drop.

I'd never had friends like Lorena and Persephone. I'd never been part of a gang, a squad. It would be nice to know that there was magic in the world, but mostly I didn't want to let my friends down, even though the very thought of doing this was ramping my anxiety back up to ten, after I'd just recently toned it back down to seven.

They were both watching me, waiting.

"Remember, Ben," Persephone said, "what you understand, you control. What you don't understand controls you."

"Okay," I said, my voice shaking. "I'll do it."

Lorena threw her arms around me and hugged me hard enough to empty the air from my lungs. When she finally stepped back, I stuck out my trembling hand, palm down, so we could do one of those *Three Musketeers* things where you put your hands on top of each other.

Persephone made a face. "Yeah, let's skip the *Fantastic*

Four hand thing."

"Definitely," Lorena chimed in.

"It's *Three Musketeers*," I said.

"Let's skip it anyway," Persephone said. "It's cringy."

I let my hand drop. "Suddenly everyone's too cool for the *Three Musketeers* thing."

Persephone knelt and unfolded her map of the surveillance cameras on the campus. "Now I just need to figure out a route into that building where we're never visible to any of the cameras."

CHAPTER 17

We strolled toward the movie theater as if we were in no particular hurry, talking about nothing in particular, waving to passing classmates.

Persephone glanced around. "When I break off, follow directly behind me. Walk where I walk. Single file."

My heart was *thump-a-thump*ing a techno beat, but I kept a smile on my face, like I didn't have a care in the world.

"Where are you going?" an unmistakable voice called. Eve was hurrying to catch up to us, her thick, powerful legs covering the ground quickly.

"Um, we're going to, um—" I tried to think of

somewhere Eve wouldn't want to go, but my mind was a blank.

"To study for tomorrow's test," Persephone blurted.

"Why?" Eve asked. It was a good question. We hadn't cracked a book in weeks.

"Ms. Spain got on us because our grades are so bad," Persephone said.

Eve studied Persephone's face as we walked. "Why are you lying?"

Could she *smell* when we were lying? Or maybe she had senses we didn't even have? Maybe she could see the carbon dioxide that came out of our mouths and it looked different when we lied. Then again, it wasn't a very good lie. None of us had shown the least bit of interest in schoolwork since we'd arrived. Ms. Spain hadn't even shown much interest.

"I think we have to tell her," Lorena said.

Persephone threw his hands in the air. "Well obviously, now that you've said that." We'd agreed not to tell Eve what we were doing until after we'd done it. We were afraid she might accidentally do something to give us away.

"Tell me what?" Eve asked.

Persephone gestured for us to follow. She led us to a spot behind our dorm, near the air-conditioning unit.

"We think we've figured out a way to snoop around the offices without being seen," Persephone said. "We're going to see if we can find out about you."

"We were planning to tell you everything we found," Lorena added. "Honest."

"I want to go," Eve said.

Persephone shook her head vigorously. "No, Eve, that won't work. We're going to try to slip through their surveillance and hope they don't notice we're gone. If *you* dropped out of sight, they'd notice immediately."

Eve crossed her short arms and made a low hiss. "But I want to help."

Three kids appeared around the corner of the building, heading toward us on the brick path. When they spotted Eve, they veered off at the next fork and headed in a different direction.

"You can help by going to the movie and acting like nothing's wrong," I said.

Eve made a noise that came from deep in her belly. "That's not helping."

"Hang on," Lorena grabbed my arm. "She could create a diversion. If Eve has a meltdown, they'll all be watching *her* instead of us."

Persephone's big eyes grew even wider. "Could you do that? Pretend to get angry about something? Flip out a little?"

"But make sure no one gets hurt," I added.

Eve lifted her arm and sucked on one of her fingers, considering. "Sometimes the popcorn at the bottom of the bucket is burnt. That could make me angry."

Lorena pumped her fist. "Perfect. Wait about twenty minutes, then make some noise."

As Eve eagerly headed off on her mission, we strolled along the back of our dormitory.

"Nice call," Persephone said over her shoulder. "For a minute there I thought the whole plan was about to unravel." She hung a sharp left and led us along the side of the cafeteria. Through the bank of windows, I could see the tables set for dinner.

Persephone stopped at the corner and consulted her map. "This way." She cut diagonally past a fountain I hadn't noticed before, shaped like a giant drinking fountain, then along a brick garden wall . . . and then right across the quad.

"They can't see us *here*?" I whispered as we crossed the wide-open expanse.

"Shh. That's right."

Weird. As we approached the center of the quad, Persephone made a sharp left, toward the administration building. She led us the long way around the building into Tulipville, where we picked our way through a bed of butter yellow tulips, avoiding the brick paths completely. We reached the edge of the building and pressed close to the rough concrete wall until we reached the back door.

Persephone peered through the window in the door. "All clear. Let's go." We ducked inside into the short hallway that intersected the main hallway.

Footsteps clopped down the main hallway, growing louder. We scrambled, each of us pressing up inside a doorway, making ourselves as flat as possible. I closed my eyes, which was stupid because it didn't make me less visible, but I couldn't help it.

The footsteps faded. I exhaled.

We tiptoed to the corner. Holding up one hand, signaling us to hang back, Persephone peered around the corner.

She waved us on.

The first office had a smoked glass window, and we could see it was dark inside. Persephone tried the knob. It was locked. So was the second door. Evidently, Persephone hadn't thought past getting inside the building unseen. Now that we were in, it wasn't like people just left their doors unlocked. Even if we found one that wasn't locked, what were the odds there were things inside that would tell us what Eve was and why we were here?

A familiar voice drifted from a partially open door halfway down the hall. Ms. Spain. She seemed like a good target. The problem was, how were we going to get inside her office?

There was a bathroom just beyond Ms. Spain's office. I cracked the door and listened: no sounds. We ducked inside.

"Seems like Ms. Spain's office is our best bet," I

whispered, "But how do we get inside?"

"I'll bet as soon as Eve starts up, she'll get word and take off," Persephone said.

"But she'll close the door on the way out, don't you think?" I asked. It seemed likely these doors locked automatically when you closed them. Since lock picking was not a skill taught in your average gifted program in middle school, that option was off the table. I tried to think of another way into Ms. Spain's office.

Muffled voices rose in the hallway. Without a word, the three of us piled into the single stall and locked it, just as the door squealed open. Through a crack between the steel panels of the stall, I watched Principal Winn pass us, heading for the urinal. A moment later, he stopped at the sink to wash his hands. We stood perfectly still. If he so much as glanced under the stall door, he'd see three pairs of scuffed tennis shoes, and we'd be doomed.

Principal Winn shut off the water and grabbed a paper towel on the way out.

We piled out of the stall.

"Wait." Persephone was staring at the base of the wall. I followed her gaze, but there was nothing there. She went and squatted at the base of the wall, then fiddled with a doorstop that was there to keep the door from slamming into the wall when people opened it.

A moment later, she stood holding the little rubber tip of the doorstop. "If we set this at the bottom of the door frame, it'll block the door from shutting. If Ms. Spain is in a hurry, she'll just pull the door closed behind her and keep going. She won't notice if the door doesn't shut completely."

Lorena slapped her forehead. "Girl. You're brilliant."

In a million years, I never would have thought of that. "You'd make a good CIA agent."

"You guys stay here." Persephone poked her head out, looked up and down the hallway, then slipped out.

Lorena and I stood as still as statues, waiting.

Persephone slipped back into the bathroom. "Done. Now we just need Eve to come through."

Persephone had told Eve to wait twenty minutes. It felt as if more than that had already passed, but it was possible time was moving slowly because of how nervous I was.

After what seemed like another twenty minutes but was probably only two, we heard a shout, then a shouted reply, followed by the *click-clop* of people running down the hall in dress shoes. When the hall grew quiet again, we ducked out of the bathroom and headed for Ms. Spain's office.

Her door looked closed, but when Lorena pushed it, it swung open. We hurried inside. I eased the door shut behind us.

"Score. She didn't have time to log out." Persephone moused over files on Ms. Spain's computer. One section consisted of all video files, labeled with dates going back ten years. Persephone turned the volume down and clicked on one at random.

A younger, smaller Eve was sitting behind a glass partition, wearing a white hospital gown. There was another being who looked just like Eve standing behind her, watching. Or maybe the one watching was Eve—it was hard to tell them apart.

"That must be Adam." Lorena tapped the seated figure. Evidently she could tell them apart.

"Concentrate," a voice said from off screen. "Remember, if you can't solve the puzzle, you don't get lunch. It's Eve's favorite—pizza—so try your hardest."

Persephone closed the file. She scrolled to an early one and clicked on it.

Four baby Eves lay in identical cribs. A younger Mr. Pierre, still with a goatee, his hair more brown than gray, was standing over one of the big barrel-shaped, plum-skinned infants, holding a photo of a woman.

"The gaze-tracking software still isn't working," someone else in the room said. "Their visual systems are just too divergent from ours."

"Then we'll do it the old-fashioned way," Mr. Pierre said. "Get a timer, and come over here and time how long she gazes at each photo."

"Try something else," Lorena suggested. "We don't have much time."

Persephone closed the video and opened a folder labeled *Medical*. Some of the file names made my skin crawl. *Susceptibility to Pathogens, Pain Tolerance, Exploratory Surgery.*

Lorena pointed. "What about *Physiology*? That might explain what she is."

Except the entire file was in medical speak, so it was hard to understand. Blood composition, descriptions of Eve's organs and what functions they served, something called BfR genomic comp. Persephone printed out a copy of the file.

There were files on each of their personalities, what made them angry and violent, what scared them, intelligence tests. Nothing that flat out said, *This is what they are*, or *This is where they came from*.

"What's this?" Persephone clicked on a folder labeled *Students*. Inside were files on each of us. Persephone clicked on her name. Inside were test scores, family history, how often Persephone had gotten in trouble at school, even video of Persephone at school, taken from a hidden camera in one of her classes.

"We're running out of time." My forehead was drenched with fear-sweat. My jaw was quivering slightly. "By the time we hear them in the hall, it'll be too late."

"Yeah," Lorena said. "We should probably get out of here."

Persephone muttered under her breath. She clicked

on a few files at random, scanning the contents before moving on to the next.

"Persephone, we gotta go." I stepped toward the door. Out in the hall, a door *thunked* closed. "Now. *Right now.*"

I took off running, with Lorena on my heels. We ducked down the side hall and pressed into a doorway just in time.

"She'll never be ready in time." I recognized Ms. Spain's voice.

"She has to be," Principal Winn said in his gravelly voice. "Whatever it takes, she has to be."

As soon as they passed, Lorena and I slipped out the back door into Tulipville beyond. We'd made it out without getting caught, but would it matter after Ms. Spain discovered Persephone in her office? I knew Persephone wouldn't sell us out, but Winn would guess we were involved.

The back door swung open. Persephone burst through it, winded from running.

"What happened?" I asked.

Persephone gestured for us to follow her farther away from the building.

"Ms. Spain followed Winn down to his office to finish the conversation they were having. As soon as their backs were turned, I bolted."

I held out my fist and Persephone gave it a bump.

We fist bumped all around, then headed off to find Eve. It was a shame we hadn't found out more about what she was, but we knew a little more, at least. Actually, what we'd overheard outside the office was more interesting than what we'd found on Ms. Spain's computer.

She's never going to be ready in time, Ms. Spain had said. Ready for what?

Beside me, Lorena burst out laughing.

I glanced at her. "What's so funny?"

"That was *awesome.*" Lorena grabbed my hand and pressed it to her upper chest. "Can you feel my heart racing."

"Wow. Yes," I said, my own pulse suddenly putting hers to shame.

She let my hand go. "We almost got nailed!"

We passed into Star Wars Park and paused in front of the Millennium Falcon fountain. I turned to Persephone. "Did Spain and Winn say anything useful after we left?"

"Winn said he thought this entire project was a mistake, that they were wasting time they couldn't afford to waste. He said he should have known better than to trust a psychologist." Persephone took a few steps to her right until the clock tower came into view. "It's seven ten. Why don't you two find Eve and tell her what we found out?"

"Where are you going?" I asked.

Persephone held up the printout she was carrying. "To see if I can decode more of the medical report."

CHAPTER 18

The high grass brushing against my bare legs was making me itchy. I should have worn long pants, even if it was warm out.

"There's no way she's going to be ready in time," Persephone repeated for the third time. "Nothing comes to mind that they could be getting you ready for?"

"I told you. *No.*" Eve was starting to lose patience. It would probably be wise for us to change the subject.

"They want something from you," Persephone said.

"I don't *have* anything. I can't *do* anything." Her voice dropped to a near whisper. "I can't even eat right."

"That's not your fault," Lorena said. "No one taught you those sorts of things when you were little. We saw the kind of stuff they put you through. It's their fault."

"What about all the weird subjects they're teaching us in this place?" I said. "I mean, etiquette? Negotiation? Foreign customs?"

"Maybe they want Eve to run for president," Lorena said.

"You have to be at least thirty-five to run for president," Persephone said.

Lorena gave Persephone a look. "I'm *joking*."

"I know. I'm just saying."

Eve's wide, froggy mouth dropped open. She pointed. "Look at *that*!"

I squinted, trying to identify what she was pointing at. It was just more tall grass.

"What is that?" Eve stalked forward. Just when I was once again beginning to wonder if her eye-ears could sense things that were invisible to me, I realized she was talking about a blue and white butterfly.

"It's a butterfly," Lorena said. "You've never seen a butterfly before?"

Eve watched the butterfly trace wild circles in the air. "I've never seen anything before." As if on cue, the butterfly flew right at Eve. It circled her head as she laugh-coughed, and it landed on her shoulder.

Lorena clapped a hand over her mouth. "That is *so* beautiful. It's like it sensed it was making you happy and came to say hello."

"Or it needed a place to land," Persephone offered.

Eve stood perfectly still, watching the butterfly slowly open and close its wings. "It smells so nice."

"It gets its food from flowers," Lorena said. "Maybe that's why."

I might have made that connection at some other time, but right now I was wrapping my mind around the fact that Eve could smell a butterfly sitting on her shoulder.

Persephone leaned in to get a closer look at the butterfly. "When they're young, butterflies are caterpillars—fuzzy worms. They transform when they reach adulthood."

"There's so much I don't know," Eve said, sounding utterly defeated.

"Don't worry about it," I said. "We'll teach you stuff."

The butterfly lifted off and flapped away. Lorena pressed her palms together and bowed her head. "Namaste, butterfly."

"What does that mean?" Eve asked.

"It means 'the eternal spirit in me bows to the eternal spirit in you.'"

"See?" I said. "We all learned something new."

Eve turned toward the quickly receding butterfly and pressed her strange, stumped hands together. "Namaste, butterfly."

We carried on walking. The point of being out in the

itchy heat was to tell Eve what we'd found out and see if she could tell us anything about her past that might connect the dots, but Eve seemed to be having such a good time just hanging out with us that I hated to break the spell.

"When I was nine, my mom bought me this butterfly kit for my birthday," I said. "You took care of the caterpillars until they turned into butterflies, and then you released them. When I opened it, I thought it was lame, but it turned out to be pretty cool." A wave of homesickness washed over me as I remembered that birthday. "I wish we could go home for the weekends. I miss home."

Lorena gave me a warning look. We walked in silence for a moment before I remembered that Eve had no home, no family. If we went home on weekends, she'd stay here alone. Or be taken back to that lab.

"Maybe when this is over, you can come visit me, Eve," I said, trying to cover my gaffe. "Persephone and Lorena too. We could have a sleepover. That's where you watch movies and play video games all night while you gorge on junk food."

"You would let me come to your house?" Eve sounded stunned.

"Sure. You'd like my dad and stepmom. My stepbrother and stepsisters can be okay sometimes." Wouldn't that be something, if I brought Eve home for a visit? No one would be forgetting I was part of the family then, would they?

"Can we go *now*?" Eve asked.

"Well, no. It would have to be once we're out of this place." I gestured at the security fence rising to our right.

Eve studied the fence, hands on hips. "I can get through that fence. Let's go now. All four of us. I want to stay up and eat junk food and watch *Star Wars* all night."

"We can't go now. One day, though." I'd meant it more as a *what if* than a formal invitation.

"No, not one day. I want to go now. I want to go *now*."

I gestured at the massive fence ringing the compound. "And I'd be happy to take you, if it wasn't for that." It was made of black, steel wire that was much thicker than your average chain-link fence, woven in a checkered pattern.

Eve eyed the fence. "I can shred that."

"Even if you could, there are armed soldiers patrolling the woods." Persephone gestured toward the campus. "Why don't we see if they'll open some of the rides for us."

Eve strode toward the fence. "I'll shred the soldiers too."

I hurried after her. "Whoa, hang on." I reached out to put a hand on Eve's shoulder, then thought better of it. "Slow down."

"I want to go now."

"Eve, we can't go to my house now."

Lorena got in front of Eve and walked backward so she was facing Eve. "Why don't all four of us ride The Cyclone together? Wouldn't that be fun?"

Eve didn't reply. She kept walking, her head down.

"Eve, we can't just break out of here," Persephone said. "That's not how this works."

Eve reached the fence. She looked up at it as her skin *flexed*. The spiky barbs shot out all at once, spearing through her dress in dozens of places. Hissing, Eve raised her arms and slashed.

The fence rattled and shook, but it didn't give.

I let out the breath I'd been holding. "Okay. You tried. Let's go back before—"

Eve's hiss rose to a metallic shriek that set my teeth on edge and sank to my bone marrow. She threw herself at the fence.

The impact knocked her to the ground, but she'd left a foot-long gash in the fence.

She sprang up and attacked the fence with everything she had. I'd known she was fast and I'd known she was strong, but this was beyond anything I'd imagined. She slashed and kicked and kneed the fence in a blurred rage. The steel bent, twisted, and snapped.

A whole section of the fence buckled. Eve grasped a jagged end, then simultaneously yanked and spun, tearing a gaping hole in the fence.

She squeezed through the hole and disappeared into the woods.

"Eve!" Turning sideways to avoid the jagged ends, I went after her.

"Benjamin, wait!" Lorena called after me.

Eve was surprisingly fast. Her tree trunk legs drove her forward, and every so often she dropped and used an arm to propel her, like a gorilla. Where was she going? She didn't know where my house was. She didn't know where *anything* was.

"Eve, stop!" The forest bed was mostly clear of brush and coated with red-gold pine needles. I glanced back at the sound of footsteps behind me, hoping it wasn't soldiers.

Lorena and Persephone were following.

I struggled to keep Eve's flapping lavender dress in sight as the forest began to slope downward, the trees growing thicker. In the distance, an alarm began to honk like some giant, lonely goose. Someone had discovered we'd escaped. I pushed myself to run faster.

"*Wait up*," Lorena called.

Reluctantly, I waited for them to catch up.

"Do you see her?" Persephone asked, panting, as we resumed running.

"No," I managed between breaths.

The *thump-thump-thump* of a helicopter rose from the direction of the school. A moment later a shadow blotted out the mottled sunlight that filtered through the pine trees. The sound grew almost deafening. The helicopter passed right over us, flying just above the treetops.

"We are in so much trouble," I shouted over the din.

We ran downhill, splashed through an icy-cold stream, and scrambled up the far bank.

I stopped running. Eve was waiting in a small clearing on the other side. She was just standing there, arms dangling at her sides. "Which way is your house?"

"Eve, it's a *hundred* miles—"

Two soldiers burst through the foliage behind Eve, rifles pointed at us.

"*Don't move,*" one of them barked.

More soldiers appeared, surrounding us. I wanted to raise my hands in the air, but he'd said not to move, so I stood perfectly still, my legs rubbery. A wind rustled the leaves overhead as the helicopter returned to hover right above us.

"*No.*" Eve shifted from one foot to the other. "*No. I want a sleepover.*"

I motioned with my hands, patting the air. "Eve, calm down. Let's not—"

With a shriek, Eve charged the nearest soldier.

The soldier aimed his rifle and fired. There was no *bang*. Just a sound like an arrow traveling through the air. It was a tranquilizer gun.

Eve made it three steps before she dropped to the forest floor. She rose to her hands and knees, struggled to stand, then collapsed facedown on the forest floor.

Four soldiers raced to Eve's still form. They lifted her and ran full tilt in the direction of the compound.

"Purple Girl is down," a soldier shouted into a walkie-talkie. "Repeat, Purple Girl is down and in transit to infirmary."

Principal Winn came on the walkie-talkie. "Understood. Detain her accomplices. Bring them to me."

"We are in so much trouble," I said under my breath.

CHAPTER 19

I tried the knob on the door for the thousandth time, then flopped back onto the cot. The room wasn't quite a prison cell, but it did the job just as well. I was starving. I didn't know what time it was, but it was definitely way past lunch time. Maybe past dinner time as well.

It bugged me that Winn hadn't let us tell our side of the story. He probably thought we'd convinced Eve to tear a hole in the fence so we could escape.

I kept expecting my mother to show up at the door to take me home. The weird thing was, I didn't want to go home. If I went home now, I'd never know what Eve was, and I might never see Lorena and Persephone again. Or Eve, for that matter.

The door creaked open. I sat up, thinking maybe it was my lunch being delivered, until I caught a glimpse of Principal Winn's buzz-cut head. Principal Winn had traded his suit for a military uniform with brass buttons, stars on the shoulders, and a series of colorful commendation patches above the pocket.

He took a seat on a stool by the door and propped one foot on the cot. "You may have forced us into a disastrous situation. But what were we doing relying on a bunch of twelve-year-olds in the first place?"

"I'm thirteen." I didn't have an answer for him. I felt sick. "Are you sending me home?"

Winn folded his arms. "You'd like that, wouldn't you? Screw everything up, then run home and hide under your bed and play with your *Star Wars* figures." The pleasant tone he'd used in our first meeting had completely vanished, replaced by a clipped, authoritarian growl.

"You're in the military?" It seemed so obvious now that I saw him in a uniform. The buzz cut, the stiff, square-shouldered way he walked.

"I figured we should drop the charade of being school administrators after the Special Forces made their appearance." He tapped the stars on his shoulder. "*General* Winn, US Army. Ms. Spain is Colonel Spain. Pierre is still Dr. Pierre. An ivory tower intellectual like him would never cut it in the military."

"Does this mean you're going to tell us what's going on?"

General Winn stabbed a finger in my direction. "What's going on is classified, and twelve-year-olds don't possess the security clearance to receive classified information. So stop asking."

I huffed in frustration. "Okay. I'll stop asking. And I'm thirteen." I was so tired and hungry. I wanted to see my friends.

"Here is all you need to know: Eve is refusing to attend class and won't speak to anyone. All the progress we've made has apparently been lost, and time is running out." I opened my mouth to speak, but Winn raised a finger. "Don't ask. You don't want time to run out. None of us wants time to run out." General Winn let that sink in for a moment. "The only thing Eve will say is that she wants to go to your house and have a movie night and eat popcorn."

I sighed and closed my eyes. "We were talking about being homesick, and I realized Eve had no home to be sick for, so I mentioned that maybe *one day, when this is over*, she could visit my house. I was trying to make her feel included, like you asked."

General Winn waved his hand around. "At this point, the 'why' doesn't matter. Thanksgiving break is four days away. We're going to start it early. Eve is going to spend the break with you and your mother, eating popcorn and watching movies."

I sprang from the cot. "*What?*" I didn't want to spend

five days with Eve. And at my *mother's* house? No.

"You're the one person she *might* talk to. You opened your big mouth and backed us all into a corner. Now it's on you."

"I usually spend Thanksgiving at home, with my father and stepmother."

"Not this Thanksgiving." General Winn stood. "You need to convince her that we're the good guys, that we have her best interests at heart."

"Who's 'we'?"

He ticked names off on his fingers. "Me, Colonel Spain, Dr. Pierre. But more generally, people. *Adults*, especially. Your mother has already given her okay. You'll be under heavy supervision at all times to minimize risk."

I tried to imagine taking Eve to the soccer facility Mom always made me go to for lessons when I was visiting her. Armed soldiers following a few paces behind us. *Everyone, this is Eve. Don't upset her, or barbs will come out of her, and she'll cut you with them. Okay, who wants to cover Eve?*

Was this guy out of his mind?

"Can Lorena and Persephone come with us?" I asked. "We work well as a team."

General Winn shook his head. "We think one-on-one is your best chance to win her over." The tight, clenched-jaw expression melted from his face for a moment, replaced by wide eyes and a slack mouth. "You have to win her over, Benjamin. You *have* to." He turned and hurried out of the room, leaving the door open behind him. I took that to mean I should follow. Evidently, I was going to my mom's. Wait until Mom met Eve.

CHAPTER 20

"Mom is a dork," I said to Eve over the buzzing of the helicopter's rotors. "She's a CIA agent, but I can't picture her chasing a criminal through a back alley. She works in the cybercrime division, so most of her criminal chasing probably takes place online. But I don't know, because she doesn't talk about her job."

The Y of the three rivers came into view out the window of the helicopter, with downtown Pittsburgh in the crook of the Y.

My palms were sweating. I'd gotten sort of used to being around Eve at the school, but there, I'd always had Lorena and Persephone with me. I didn't know how it was going to go, being alone with Eve. For days.

The city moved out of sight behind us, replaced by suburban houses and stores. I spotted Publix, a long rectangle surrounded on three sides by pavement. Vehicles scooted around the parking lot, looking like matchboxes. I traced Larimer Avenue past the fire station, to Mom's neighborhood, looking for her house.

When I spotted it, I was confused by the thick line running along the edges of the property. None of the other houses had one. As we got closer, I could make out what it was: they'd erected a steel fence around our property, just like the one around Sagan Middle School. I'd been wondering how we were supposed to explain Eve to Mom's neighbors. The answer was, we weren't, because they weren't going to see her. Soldiers with rifles roamed inside the fence. A few dozen of her neighbors were standing outside the fence, probably wondering what the heck was going on. They must have been awfully confused and curious, seeing as the military had shown up and erected a huge fence around the house .

For the thousandth time, I wondered what could be so important about Eve that the government would devote this much attention to her.

She's never going to be ready in time, Dr. Pierre had said. Ready for what?

Mom was waiting as our helicopter set down on the front lawn. It felt like I hadn't seen her in a year, although it had only been five weeks.

As a soldier helped us out of the copter, Eve eyed Mom suspiciously, the puckers in her skin turning to bulges, her barbs threatening to erupt. She was my mom, but she was still an adult. A tall, gawky, knock-kneed adult with a red nose and squinty eyes, but an adult nonetheless.

Mom shifted from foot to foot, looking like she didn't know what to do with her hands. I figured it was up to me to do the introductions, so I said, "Mom, this is Eve."

Mom surged forward. "It's an honor to meet you, Eve." She shook Eve's fingers correctly, like it was something she did all the time, but I could see her hand shaking. "That's a beautiful dress."

It was exactly the right thing to say. I could almost feel the pleasure radiating off Eve as she said, "I choose what I'm going to wear each day myself."

"Well, you have great taste." Mom turned to me. She gave me a fierce hug, and whispered into my ear, "I'm proud of you."

I broke off the hug and put some space between us. I was not happy that she'd risked my life sending me to that school and had put me in the position I was currently in.

"A little birdie told me you're a big pizza fan," Mom said to Eve. "So I picked up a pie from Mr. Pizza."

"Mr. Pizza is *the best*," I said. "Wait till you taste it.

The cafeteria's pizza is garbage compared to this."

"I'd like to try some. I'm *very* hungry," Eve said.

Mom clapped her hands together. "Then let's have some Mr. Pizza. Since Eve is our guest, she gets to pick a movie to watch while you eat."

I tried to mask my surprise. I was *never* allowed to watch TV during dinner when I was at Mom's house.

One of the soldiers, a tall Latina woman with a buzz cut and a big smile, hurried to open the front door for us. "Welcome. I'm Maria. If there's anything you need—and I mean anything—just ask one of us soldiers and we'll see that you get it. We're all here for you to make sure you're safe, and happy, and have a great Thanksgiving."

"Um, thanks," I said, confused. In movies, soldiers were stone-faced and serious, while this one sounded like a cross between a tour guide and a butler.

As soon as we were inside, Eve stopped and looked around. "I have to go to the bathroom."

"It's right over there, sweetheart." Mom pointed down the hall.

As the bathroom door closed, Mom gave my shoulder a squeeze and whispered, "I'm sorry. I know this is hard on you."

A *crash* came from the bathroom. Mom and Maria the soldier both bolted in that direction.

"Hang on." I ran after them, waving my arms. "It's okay. *Stop.*"

They stopped and waited anxiously for an explanation.

"She breaks mirrors. It's . . . just something she does."

"Oh." Mom shrugged. "All right."

Eve appeared in the doorway.

"Why don't we go to the basement and wait for the pizza?" I suggested.

Eve followed me down to my favorite room, my refuge. The shelves in the basement were filled with books and spillover from my comics, action figures, and trading cards collection, which I mostly kept at Dad's. There was an old sofa in the middle of the room and a mega-screen TV mounted on the wall.

I turned on the TV and scrolled to *Star Wars* Episode IV. The familiar music and the scroll of words through space at the opening calmed me a little. This wasn't so bad. Yes, Eve could tear me to ribbons if she wanted, but why would she?

There were a few little cuts on her arm from when she'd smashed the mirror, one oozing a few drops of bright white blood. Maybe if I understood why some things made her angry, I could avoid unintentionally triggering her?

"Can I ask you something?" I said to Eve.

"Yes."

"How come you smash mirrors?"

Eve's skin started to bulge, her barbs coming close enough to the surface that it looked as if the tips of nails were poking out all over her. I leaned away from her, ready to flee.

The barbs slowly settled back into her skin. "I don't want to see myself."

"Oh." It seemed cruel to act like it was perfectly understandable that Eve wouldn't want to see herself, so I added, "Why is that?"

The silence stretched on, as a young Luke Skywalker shopped for droids.

Eve finally spoke in a voice I could barely hear. "There was a woman who used to clean the lab outside our cage. Sometimes she would cry while she cleaned. Sometimes to pass the time, Adam and me made up stories of why she was so sad. Then one day we heard her tell the supervisor she couldn't come to clean anymore. She said we were so ugly we gave her nightmares."

The words took my breath away. "What a terrible thing to say. You look different from most people, but that doesn't mean you're ugly." I struggled for words. I wished Lorena was here—she was so much better at talking about beauty and magic and that sort of thing. I tried to imagine what she would say. "You're a special person, Eve. You're beautiful in your own unique way."

Eve rose from the couch. She turned her back to me. "I can see myself. I know what I look like."

"Beauty is mostly a made-up thing anyway. A bunch of people get together and agree that small noses are more beautiful than big ones, that tall is better than short, that thin is better than fat. I think you look fine. I—I *like* the way you look."

Eve twisted her head almost completely backward to look at me. She didn't have a neck. When she turned her head, the entire top of her body twisted. She studied my face.

I wasn't being honest—not completely honest, anyway. But it also wasn't a total lie, it wasn't something I was saying just to protect Eve's feelings. I was getting used to the way she looked. The more I saw her, the more she just looked like Eve. My guess was, after seeing her for a long enough time, she wouldn't seem the least bit weird or repulsive. She'd just look like Eve.

Eve turned to the TV screen. "Who is that?" Evidently the conversation was over. Hopefully I'd helped her feel a little better about the way she looked.

As we watched, it suddenly struck me that in a weird, fun-house sort of way, this was what I'd always wished for: having a friend to hang out with, someone who called for no reason or showed up at the door unannounced. Someone who didn't treat our friendship as an afterthought. I just hadn't pictured someone quite as strange and potentially dangerous as Eve.

CHAPTER 21

I set my bowl of popcorn on the table as quietly as possible. Eve's head was lolling back onto the couch cushion, her wide mouth open, her hissing breath steady and even. I waved at her to make sure she was asleep. It was hard to tell with her odd eyes.

I tiptoed up the basement stairs toward the kitchen, where I could hear Mom on the phone.

"I've got a nasty bump on the back of my head," she was saying, probably to Aunt Liz. She used a different tone when she talked to Aunt Liz—less serious adult, more sister. "No. Yes. He said the combination of the anxiety meds and exhaustion probably caused me to pass out."

I froze, my fingers inches from the doorknob, feeling guilty for having overheard something I wasn't supposed to hear. Anxiety meds? Exhaustion? I backed down the stairs quietly, trying to make sense of what I'd overheard. Mom was always on top of everything, always prepared, bulletproof in her perfectly tailored suits. Nothing rattled Mom.

Or did she just hide it well so I would feel like she had everything under control? She'd passed out and hit her head because she was exhausted.

I listened to the murmur of Mom's voice, too far away now to eavesdrop, until she finally hung up.

I tiptoed back upstairs.

She was sitting at the kitchen table, a steaming cup of herbal tea in front of her. I pulled up the chair across from her, and Mom gave me a big, bright smile that didn't quite reach her eyes. "Where is Eve?"

"She fell asleep. It's been a big day for her, I guess. It's the first time she's been anywhere but the school and the lab."

Mom got a plate piled with oatmeal chocolate chip cookies she'd baked and set them in front of me. I was stuffed from all the popcorn, but I took one anyway, because they're awesome, and because Mom had taken the time to make them, and I needed to go easier on her from now on.

I bit into the cookie, which was still gooey-soft.

"She's been a prisoner in a lab her whole life."

"I know. They briefed me."

I sat up. "What else did they tell you? Do you know what Eve is?"

Mom shook her head. "That's above my pay grade."

"What do you *think* she is?"

Mom took a sip of tea. From the look on her face, it was still too hot. Or maybe it was my question that made her flinch. "I'm not sure I could even venture a guess. What I do know is she's extremely important. Lives are at stake. Many lives. They told me that much. Somehow, we have to convince Eve she can trust us. Not just you and your friends. All of us."

"Why *us*? Why do *we* have to convince her?"

Mom shook her head slowly, ponderously. "I guess because Eve chose you."

I set my half eaten cookie on the plate. "Mom, why would you trust people who won't even tell you what you are and where you came from? If they want Eve's trust, they have to trust *her*."

Mom cupped her palm over her eyes. It was a habit she had when she was frustrated. "I'm sure they have a good reason for not telling her. These people are from the highest echelons of the government. They know what they're doing."

I made a grunting sound. She sounded like Grace and Lucian. "You *must* have a lot of faith in them, to send your own son there."

Mom looked startled. "I did it because I have a lot of faith in *you*,"

"Is that why I'm living with Dad, because you have a lot of faith in me?" Immediately, I regretted saying it. Mom looked devastated. I'd just overheard her saying she'd passed out from exhaustion, and here I was making it worse.

"My job takes up so much of my time," she stammered. "I wouldn't have been able to take care of you. You'd be alone all the time. I've told you that."

The basement door squeaked open. Eve stepped partway out, then paused, her hand on the knob.

I jumped up and pulled out the seat next to me. "Come and join us. I was just telling Mom how homesick I was in the first weeks away from home. I was so terrified to be on my own." And terrified of her, but she didn't need to hear that.

Eve padded into the kitchen on her big, round, bare feet, her plum-colored toes sticking out partway up her shins. "Today was the first day in my life I wasn't terrified."

Her words jolted me. I'd never thought of Eve as scared of anything, only angry.

"I wish I could live here all the time." Eve turned to Mom. "If you would be my mother, and Benjamin and Adam were my brothers, I'd never be scared again."

I swallowed, choking back tears. Even with Eve's strange voice, her pain and longing was so clear, so raw. I could relate. *Today was the first day in my life I wasn't terrified.* I understood what it was like to be scared all the time, to never feel okay. She'd had good reasons to be terrified, while mine had mostly been about a faulty anxiety setting in my brain, but I got what it felt like. It sucked.

The kitchen chair squeaked on the tile as Mom stood. She went to Eve, and you could have blown me over with a fan when she gently put a hand on Eve's shoulder. "I'd like that too, Eve. But it's not up to me. It's up to General Winn because he's your legal guardian. Maybe if we're all nice to him, he'll agree to let you live here."

I gawked at my mother. What the heck was going on? Who was this woman? Had my mother just suggested she would be willing to adopt Eve, and if so, that I would live here as well? Hadn't she just told me she was too busy with her job to have me living here? Yet if Eve lived here too, suddenly she wasn't too busy? I liked Eve, and I didn't like living in a house with three kids who barely acknowledged I was there, but that didn't mean I wanted to live in the same house with a girl who cut people when she got angry.

And how would it even work? I tried to picture Eve riding the school bus to middle school. The other kids might eventually get used to the way she looked, but their parents would never let them ride to school with a spiky, unpredictable being of unknown origin.

"General Winn is my father?" Eve asked.

Mom sat. "I don't think he's your father, sweetie. A guardian is the person who makes decisions for you until you're an adult. It doesn't have to be a parent."

"A guardian owns you," Eve said. "And can do terrible things to you."

Eve waited for one of us to say something. I didn't know what to say. I thought of that video I'd seen with Lorena and Persephone, the voice telling Eve and Adam that if they didn't solve the puzzle, they wouldn't get lunch. From what Eve had said, there were worse things on those videos. Much worse.

Mom's voice was gentle and sad. "I think he's sorry for what he did."

"Then maybe he should apologize," I blurted.

Mom nodded. "Maybe he should." In the bright kitchen light, the lines around her eyes seemed deeper than usual.

There was a heaviness in the air, none of us sure of what to say. I tried to think of something that would give us all a lift. Especially Eve. It must be hard to find out your legal guardian was the person who'd kept you locked in a cage your whole life.

"Maria the soldier said we could have anything we wanted, that all we had to do was ask. Let's ask for something."

Eve touched her belly. "I'm hungry again."

I tried to think of a food that would brighten our moods—something that would make the evening an event, a party. "Mom, remember those gigantic peanut butter, banana, and bacon submarine sandwiches we got at that restaurant in Philadelphia?"

Eve half stood. "They sound delicious."

Mom gave me a *don't be ridiculous* look. "Benjamin, they're not going to travel three hundred miles to pick up *sandwiches*."

"I don't know. Maybe they would." They'd erected an entire amusement park to make Eve happy. Surely they'd pick up a few sandwiches on the other side of Pennsylvania.

I jumped up, feeling bold because I was Eve's closest friend, and everything revolved around Eve. "I'm going to go ask."

Mom *tsked* at me, but she didn't say I couldn't. I ran to find a soldier.

Maria the soldier was standing guard on the front porch, her arms folded behind her back. "Hey, Benjamin. Is there something I can do for you?"

"There is something, but it's kind of crazy."

Maria shrugged. "Depends on what kind of crazy it is. We can't do anything that might put Eve or you in any sort of danger."

I waved my hands. "It's nothing like that. It's just,

I was telling Eve about these incredible peanut butter, banana, and bacon sandwiches we once got from this famous restaurant in Philadelphia, and she really wants to try one. I know it's—"

Maria raised her hand. "I know the place you're talking about. It's called The Foundry. Those sandwiches are *awesome*." She lifted her walkie-talkie to her mouth. "Purple Bird, we have a request for . . ." She lowered the walkie-talkie. "Does your mom want one, or just you and Eve?"

I hadn't thought to ask Mom. "She wants one too." If she didn't want it, I was pretty sure Eve would happily eat it.

Maria raised her walkie-talkie. "We have a request for three peanut butter, banana, and bacon sandwiches from The Foundry in Philly. In fact, pick one up for me too. I'll pay you back."

The walkie-talkie crackled. "Roger that. Four P-B-and-Bs. Plus another for me, and I'm guessing we'll be up to about a dozen once word gets around."

"Roger that." Laughing, Maria signed off as a chopper rose into the air from behind the fence.

"I'm guessing you'll have your sandwiches in about ninety minutes," Maria said. "Is there anything else I can do for you?"

"No, that's it. Thank you. Thank you so much." I headed back inside, grinning, and feeling a little stunned.

CHAPTER 22

Eve had peanut butter all over her chin and cheeks, but she looked happy as she took another Eve-sized bite of the sub. I'd made it through less than half of mine, which was still almost a foot of sandwich. It wasn't just long, it was thick. I propped my feet on the old coffee table and watched the movie.

I couldn't say I was enthralled by it. It was about a twelve-year-old girl name Piper who runs away from home, buys a bunch of makeup and clothes, and passes as a grown woman. Eve seemed mesmerized by it, though. She was leaning all the way forward in her seat, watching the girl's every move, hanging on every word as she chewed.

I stifled a yawn as, on the screen, the girl pushed a cart through Walmart, stopping at a rack of cheap earrings. She picked out a pair and tossed them in her cart.

Eve pointed at the screen. "I want those. I want earrings like those." She looked at me. I wasn't sure if she expected me to spring up and get her some, or what.

"I want earrings," she repeated.

"After the movie's over, we can ask Maria to send someone out to get you some."

Eve shook her head vigorously. Except, because she had no neck, the whole top of her torso moved with her head. "I want to buy them *myself*. In a store, the way Piper did."

Like a normal kid. I couldn't blame her. "You must be sick of not being able to do what you want. To go where you want."

Eve set her sandwich down on the snack tray, missing her plate completely. "I've never been anywhere. I've never done anything."

"Maybe the general will take us on a field trip to Walmart if we ask," I joked.

"I want to go to Walmart." Eve said *Walmart* in a reverent tone, the way a six-year-old might say *Disneyland*. "Please. *Please*."

She deserved a trip to Walmart. She deserved a trip to Disneyland, to the *moon*, after the childhood she'd had. But we weren't allowed to leave the property. Even if we could sneak off and make it to Walmart, someone would call the police the minute Eve walked in the door.

"I want to buy earrings and pay for them myself."

"I'd like to take you, I honestly would. But there are guards everywhere. Remember what happened when you tried to leave the school?"

"They shot me," Eve growled.

"Well, they shot you with tranquilizers, but I'm sure it still sucked."

She pressed her purple fingers to the sides of her head. "I had a terrible headache when I woke."

I nodded in sympathy, and we went back to watching the movie. I could see Eve's heart wasn't in it anymore. Every so often, almost like she was saying it for the first time, she announced that she wanted to go to Walmart.

It started to annoy me. I mean, we'd brought her to my house, fed her pizza and peanut butter, bacon, and banana sandwiches, let her pick the movies, and now all she could do was complain about the thing we *couldn't* do.

As I watched her out of the corner of my eye, I started to feel guilty for being annoyed. She'd had a terrible life so far. What must it have been like to grow up with no adult you could count on, no one in the world who cared about you except your brother, if that's what Adam was? Even though my parents were divorced, I'd always been surrounded by adults who loved me. What if none of those people existed, and I had grown up a prisoner in a hospital? I watched Eve forlornly watching the movie. She was entitled to a lot of slack. I had to keep that in mind.

Eve caught me looking at her. "Please, Benjamin. Please." It was impossible to read that face, but I didn't need to. This was terribly important to her for some reason—the most important thing in the world. I think she was wondering if she could really count on me, if I really was her friend, or if she was on her own as always.

"I'll try to figure it out—" Eve leaped up in her seat, full of hope. I raised my finger. "—but I can't promise anything. I'm not sure there's a way to sneak you out of this place. It's like a fortress."

"We'll figure it out," Eve said.

She needed a disguise. Maybe a big hoodie and some sunglasses. She'd have to keep her head down and her blueberry-colored hands in her pockets. And she couldn't speak. It was hard to get Eve to follow directions, though. She was a total loose cannon.

I turned to Eve. "If I can figure out how to get us to Walmart, do you promise you'll keep quiet and keep your head down? I'd have to hand the money to the cashier, but you could hold it in your pocket until I do."

Eve held out her hand. "Deal."

I shook her fingers, just like I'd learned on the first day of class. Now I just had to figure out how to sneak Eve past a perimeter of professional soldiers.

CHAPTER 23

From my bedroom window, I watched as a soldier swung open the front gate. An olive green Hummer SUV pulled through. General Winn's buzz-cut profile was unmistakable in the passenger seat, sending an instinctive stab of revulsion through me. Now that I knew he'd been in charge of Eve through her awful childhood, I didn't like him. I didn't trust him.

As the Hummer headed around the corner toward the back of the house, I studied its back end. It had a big, roomy hatch back, and the windows were heavily tinted.

A wonderful, terrifying thought occurred to me. If someone were to hide back there under a blanket, they would be hard to spot. And who was going to search a general's vehicle?

I glanced over at Eve, a blanket-covered lump still asleep on the double-wide cot the soldiers had brought for her. She would definitely fit.

I swallowed, my mouth already bone-dry at the thought of actually doing what I was contemplating. I hurried to the bathroom because, big surprise, suddenly I had the runs just thinking about doing this. I was not an action guy. I didn't like excitement. At all. Yet here I was, contemplating this prison break not just as an abstract idea, but as something I was really going to attempt. But I'd made a promise to Eve. We'd shook on it. Somehow, I had to sneak her to Walmart.

Back in my room, I dug around in my closet, looking for something Eve could use as a disguise. "Eve, wake up." Nothing looked anywhere near big enough. I'd have to pilfer one of Mom's. I went across the hall and peered out the bathroom window into the back yard, where General Winn was stepping out of the Hummer, which was parked right beside the patio. A soldier stationed back there saluted as he passed.

I went back to my bedroom. "Eve, *come on.*" I was afraid if I shook her, her barbs might come shooting out.

"I'm not sleeping," Eve muttered from underneath the blankets.

"Well, get up, then."

Peering out of my room and looking both ways, I

darted toward Mom's room to find Eve a disguise.

@

"Remember, just agree with whatever I say," I whispered to Eve as we approached the soldier, whose hair was piled up under her army green cap. She struck me as the outdoorsy type, who spent her free time camping and kayaking and stuff. I gave her a big smile. "Excuse me, ma'am."

The soldier gave me an even bigger, toothier smile. "Hey Benjamin, afternoon Eve. You can call me Rory. What can I do for you two?"

"We were talking about how we haven't been getting much exercise these last few days, weren't we, Eve?"

"Yes," Eve said.

"And it occurred to me: wouldn't it be fun to have a trampoline park in the backyard?"

Rory's eyebrows pinched together. "A trampoline park? You mean, more than one trampoline?"

"I was thinking maybe a four-by-four grid, set just a few feet apart from each other, so you can jump from one to the next."

Rory looked uneasy. "That sounds dangerous. What if you miss? It'd be a big drop."

"No, it wouldn't, because the trampolines are at ground level. You excavate a few feet into the ground underneath them."

Rory's frown got a little deeper. "Excavate."

"That's right." I glanced at the back door. General Winn would be coming any minute. If we were still standing here when he did, we were out of luck.

Rory studied the yard, probably wondering how in the world they could excavate sixteen rectangles back there. "Let me see what I can do." She headed around the house, toward the front yard.

As soon as she was out of sight, I squeezed the latch on the rear hatch of the Hummer.

"Get in."

Eve climbed into the space. She almost filled it entirely, in fact. "Can you pull your legs in so there's room for me?"

Eve tucked her legs in as tightly as she could, but the space it opened would have barely fit a house cat.

The back door creaked open. I heard General Winn's voice.

"Shoot." I pulled Mom's oversize hoodie out from under my jacket and draped it over Eve, then scrambled over her into the back row of seats. Curling into a ball on the floor, I covered myself with the blanket I had intended to put over both of us. If General Winn glanced back from the front seat, there was no way he wasn't going to notice a blanket covering a kid-sized object.

Doors opened and slammed. The big engine growled to life.

I felt the Hummer swing a U-turn and jostle toward the front of the house before rolling to a stop.

"Have a good day, sir," the soldier at the gate said. Then we were off, hitting the smooth street and picking up speed.

"Good afternoon, Madam President," General Winn said. My already-racing heart found a higher gear. "No, I'm afraid there hasn't been much progress. Eve is less volatile, but she's just as hostile toward authority figures as when she arrived."

I was close enough to hear the faintest murmur coming through the phone. That was the president's voice. Unbelievable.

"I still think this is less about how she was treated, and more about her being fundamentally different from us. I don't think she's *capable* of empathy, of civility."

The president spoke again.

"Well, that's his opinion. I don't agree. This is a waste of precious time. We should return to the enhanced behavior modification protocol for the hours we have left. To put it bluntly, we're dealing with a psychopath, and we should approach this accordingly."

The president spoke a little louder, but not loud enough for me to hear what she said.

"Yes, Ma'am," General Winn replied. "No. We'll continue to do everything we can. Thank you. I'll be in touch at 1400 hours unless there are new developments."

Suddenly, I was less sure about this whole trip to Walmart thing, but it was too late now. Eve would never agree to go back empty-handed. That didn't make her a psychopath, though. There was a psychopath in this vehicle all right, but not in the back.

The Hummer slowed and turned in somewhere. We turned again, then pulled to a stop. The engine went silent. Doors slammed.

I counted to twenty, then pulled the blanket off and peered around. We were in the Doubletree Hotel parking lot. Maybe this was where General Winn was staying during Eve's vacation. I climbed into the middle seats and opened the door. Trying not to draw attention, I opened the back hatch.

Eve sat up.

"Put on the hoodie." I looked around. There was no one in sight. "Okay, come on out, but whatever you do, keep your head down."

I headed toward a wooded area alongside the parking lot. Walmart was about two miles away—we could stick to woods and brushy areas as much as possible.

CHAPTER 24

I studied Eve on the trash-littered bank of the stream that ran through a brush-choked gully. One glimpse of her wide, purple face and we'd get busted.

"Look down so I can't see your face, then take a few steps."

Eve did as I asked. She looked like a major appliance in a hoodie.

"Limp a little, like you're old and have a bad knee."

Eve took a few more steps, this time limping.

"That's good," I said. "It makes more sense that you're hunched over like that if you're old. Now remember, keep your hands in your pockets and don't speak." I looked her over one more time. "Are you ready?"

Eve looked around. "Where is Walmart?"

I pointed up out of the gully. "That way. Across a parking lot. But Eve, you *have* to remember to keep your head down."

"I will." She sounded impatient. I guess I couldn't blame her—I'd said the same thing about ten times.

We climbed out of the gully, pushing through brush and branches, into the Walmart parking lot. As a big semitruck rumbled past, my heart pounded. Was it immediately obvious Eve wasn't like the rest of us? I had gotten so used to the way she looked that she didn't seem all that different to me. But what about someone who'd never laid eyes on her before?

We passed a mom-aged woman pushing a shopping cart toward her car. She didn't even glance Eve's way.

"So far, so good," I said under my breath.

We passed more customers, some pushing carts, others carrying bags.

At the automatic doors, we were met by a whoosh of chilly air, then by an elderly woman greeter who looked Eve up and down, giving us a tight smile and no greeting. I veered off the main aisle between racks of clothes as soon as possible to get Eve out of sight. We wound past sweat suits, underwear, and pajamas to the jewelry section.

"Here we go." I gestured at the wall. "Look at all those great earrings." Except, I suddenly realized, you needed pierced ears to wear them. I looked around. "Here." I led Eve down the wall. "These are clip-ons."

Eve surveyed the cheap, glittery selection of gold and silver earrings. She pulled her hand out of her pocket and reached for a pair of loop earrings pinned on cardboard.

I quickly snatched down the earrings she was reaching for. "Hands in pockets, please." I held the earrings out for her. "Do you like these?"

Eve studied the earrings from the depths of the hood, then turned back toward the display without a word.

I took down a pair with emerald-colored glass at the center. "These are nice. They'd go well with your complexion." Like I knew what I was talking about. I just wanted to get out of there.

A low hiss came from Eve, rising in pitch like water boiling. It was hard to say whether she didn't appreciate my help, or thought I was making fun of the way she looked. I put the earrings back, wishing Lorena and Persephone were here. Eve would probably take another girl's advice on fashion before mine. Plus, I missed them. I missed bantering with them and having companions to help me navigate the tornado my life had become since that bus pulled through the heavily guarded gates of Sagan Middle School for High-Achieving and Obedient Kids.

Eve scanned the rows, studying each pair of earrings for an instant before moving to the next. I inhaled to ask if she was looking for something in particular, then thought better of it. The less she spoke, the better. I glanced around the store. Thankfully, no one was paying us any attention.

"*There*." Eve's neck was craned toward the top row.

"Which ones?" I touched a pair of dangly shields. "These?"

Eve shook her head.

I moved down the row, pausing with my finger on each pair until Eve nearly shouted, "*Those*."

They were shaped like silver butterflies in flight. As I took them down, I couldn't help smiling. "Perfect. Okay. Let's go." I headed for the registers.

Eve made no move to follow.

"Eve, come *on*."

Eve turned in the other direction and raised her chin. "I want to *see*."

"Another time. *Please*. We need to get going," I said.

Eve headed in the opposite direction from the doors. I hurried after her. I could understand her wanting to look around since this could be her only chance to see the outside world, but it was too risky.

"Please turn around," I whispered, trying not to attract attention. "Please, please."

Eve stopped in front of a *Star Wars* t-shirt display, her shoulders rising and falling like she was out of breath. A Rey mannequin was modeling one of the shirts, which said "Pew Pew" on it. Eve studied the neatly folded shirts stacked on a table.

"Do you want a t-shirt?" I grabbed an XXXL from the table. "I'll get you one, but you have to promise you'll go, right now."

Eve went on looking at the t-shirts. This was exactly what I'd been afraid would happen. Eve was not good at following directions.

Movement to our left caught my eye: a six- or seven-year-old girl and her father, heading our way.

"Eve, we have to go. Right now."

"Star Wars!" The girl let go of her father's hand and ran toward the display. "I love Star Wars." She squeezed between me and Eve. She looked over her shoulder at her father. "Daddy, Star Wars."

"Yes, I see," the dad said.

The little girl looked up at Eve. "Do you like Star Wars?"

"*Eve,*" I warned, as Eve looked down at the girl.

The girl screamed. She backpedaled, stumbled into me, and fell as Eve hissed, the spikes on her skin visible through the hoodie.

Her father pushed past me. "Get away from her. What *is* that?" He got between Eve and his daughter, accidentally elbowing Eve. Lightning fast, Eve's spiked hand lashed out. The father shouted in pain and surprise, clapping his hand over his forearm.

"Don't touch me." Eve's hood had fallen off.

The guy swept his daughter up in his arms and backpedaled away from Eve, blood dribbling from a gash in his forearm. "*Security! Help, we need security!*" He ran into the main aisle, shouting.

"Let's go." I led the way through the racks, avoiding the main aisle.

A woman screamed.

"Eve, *pull your hood up.*"

"*Stay where you are.*" A security guard was jogging along the main aisle, moving to intercept us.

Breaking into a run, I changed course, heading toward the back of the store. Eve knocked clothes off racks as we dodged around them.

I plowed into a gray-haired woman, nearly knocking her over.

"Sorry," I called as we kept running.

The security guard was sprinting down a wide main aisle, moving to cut us off. I changed directions as he cut into the racks toward us, yelling for us to stop. There was no way we were going to outrun him.

"Eve. Stop." I stopped, raised my hands in the air.

Eve kept going. Her hood had fallen off again. She knocked a rack of sweaters over as three shrieking teenage girls scurried out of her way.

"Eve! Stop!" She ignored me. I took off after her. The security guard was nowhere in sight.

Eve crossed the open central lane into an aisle in the toy section.

I sprinted after her. "Eve! *Stop!*"

The security guard suddenly appeared at the end of the aisle, blocking Eve's path.

Hissing like a thousand cobras, Eve charged right at him. The security guard spread his arms, ready to tackle her.

Eve hurled him into the shelves. Toys flew everywhere as the guard bounced off the shelves and dropped to the floor.

I stepped around the writhing security guard. What had I done? I should have known this would happen if I took Eve into a store. What had I been thinking? Now two people were injured. I had to get her out of the store before she hurt anyone else.

At the end of the aisle, I looked left, then right. I'd lost sight of Eve.

In the distance, I heard a shout. "*Police. Don't move.*"

"Oh no. Eve!" I headed toward the voice.

Before I'd gone more than a few steps, Eve appeared around a corner, coming right toward me.

"*Eve,*" I cried out. "*Stop. You have to stop.*"

Three police officers came hurtling around the corner after her. Two were carrying tasers.

"*On the floor,*" a voice behind us barked.

I spun. More police, with tasers. We were surrounded.

I'd seen videos of people being tased, jumping and jerking as electricity shot through them. I did *not* want to be tased.

"I'll shred you. I'll shred you all," Eve howled. Her spikes had torn through her hoodie and dress in dozens of places.

"You." A police officer with a goatee pointed at me. "Step away from it. Now."

"She's just a kid," I said. "She's upset."

"Move away. *Now*," the officer demanded, louder.

Eve spun, looking for a place to run. "I'll slash you."

"*Take it,*" the goateed officer shouted.

I stepped in front of Eve, hands raised. "*Wait.*"

Behind me, Eve shrieked in pain. She dropped to the floor, jerking. Four different wires ran from her to tasers held by the officers standing behind us.

"Stop," I screamed. "Leave her alone."

Booming shouts rose from the front of the store. Some of the officers turned to see what was happening.

Soldiers in camo fatigues, clutching automatic rifles, surged toward us from every direction at once.

"Drop your weapons," a female soldier wearing a big earpiece said. It was Maria. I didn't understand. I didn't have a weapon, and neither did Eve. I looked around, trying to understand what I was supposed to do.

Then I realized: the soldiers weren't pointing their rifles at *us*, they were pointing them at the *police*.

"Drop your weapons *immediately*," Maria repeated.

Looking incredibly confused, the officer with the goatee set his taser on the floor and showed Maria his empty hands. The rest of the police officers followed.

"What *is* this?" the officer with the goatee said.

"We're assuming control of this operation," Maria answered. Her eyes went wide as she saw Eve. "*Medic! Get the medic up here.*"

Eve wasn't moving. Not at all. It looked like she might not be breathing.

CHAPTER 25

Mom and I didn't talk as we headed across the compound toward the special medical facility hidden on the school grounds, designed and outfitted specifically for Eve's physiology. A soldier led the way while another walked behind us.

A handful of students were cutting across the quad, heading toward the cafeteria for lunch. Turned out Eve and I were the only students who'd been allowed to go home for Thanksgiving, probably because Winn and Company didn't want the other kids telling their friends and family about Eve. Because everything here was about Eve.

"I still can't wrap my mind around it," Mom said,

continuing the diatribe she'd started on the helicopter. "You think you know not only better than *me*, but better than the entire combined judgment of the US government."

"I was trying to make Eve happy, so she'll like us. Everyone says that's all that matters. And the only thing that was going to make her happy was to buy some earrings. To go to the store and buy them herself."

"Then you *ask us*. You don't *smuggle her out*. She almost died!"

"If I'm such a disaster at being her nursemaid, maybe one of you adults who knows so much should have been doing it." I would have said more, but we'd reached the entrance to the infirmary, an unmarked polished steel door in the back of a squat building on the edge of the compound.

Inside, Eve was separated from us by glass walls. She was lying in something that looked more like a cocoon than a bed, only her head visible. Her eye-ears were closed. Mom hung back, leaving me to go into her room alone.

I stood over Eve, not sure what to do. In movies, people usually said soothing things to people who were unconscious in a hospital bed, but I felt stupid talking to someone who obviously couldn't hear me.

It wasn't healthy to jolt a normal body with a ton of electricity, but for Eve's body, it was much worse. Mom told me it had something to do with how her double hearts communicated using electrical impulses so they would beat in the right rhythm, and the jolt of the taser interrupted that communication. If the soldiers hadn't shown up with a medic who understood how Eve's body worked, she would have died on the floor of that Walmart.

I felt awful about putting Eve in danger. But everyone was leaving it to me to keep Eve happy, to watch out for her, when they wouldn't tell me anything about her, not even that she had two hearts. It was too much. I felt as if I hadn't had a good night's sleep in weeks. I felt like I should be more anxious than I was—I was pretty sure I'd reached what my psychologist called adrenal exhaustion. My body just didn't have any adrenaline left to pump.

Two hearts. Was there any animal on Earth that had two hearts?

I stuck my hands in the pockets of my jacket. My fingers brushed the butterfly earrings mounted on their plastic card that I'd shoved in there as the medic had worked on Eve. Technically, it was the first thing I'd ever shoplifted, but it wasn't as if the soldiers would have waited while I paid for them. I carefully clipped them onto Eve's strange, circular ear-eyelobes.

I turned and headed back out to Mom.

"What happens now?" I asked. "Do we have class tomorrow even though Eve won't be there?"

Mom rubbed her bloodshot eyes. "I don't know. We're supposed to report to General Winn's office after you visit Eve."

I was in big trouble with Winn this time. The two soldiers assigned to us escorted us to the administration building.

Mom stayed behind as I headed into the building.

"Be good," she called after me. "Make good choices."

Winn, Colonel Spain, and Dr. Pierre were waiting for me in General Winn's office. A few months ago (which felt like ten years ago), the look General Winn gave me as I entered might have made me wet my pants. He was furious, his face crimson. He also looked exhausted—sunken-eyed and unwashed. They all did.

I didn't wait for him to start on me—I began my defense as soon as I sat down. "What should I have done, let her go to Walmart alone? Because one way or another, she was going. Maybe when she took off in the store, I should have tackled her and hoped she didn't slice me to pieces."

Winn threw back his head, closed his eyes, and huffed in frustration. "She never would have made it out of that compound without your help. You smuggled her out. You took her to a *store*. You didn't *follow* her, you *led* her into an incredibly dangerous situation. Of all the kids she could have befriended. You have *no idea* what you risked."

"You're right. I don't. I have no idea, because you won't tell me." I folded my arms across my chest.

Finally, Colonel Spain said, "He's the only one she trusts. Maybe if he trusted us, we'd get somewhere."

"I agree," Dr. Pierre said to the general. "That's two to one. *Three* to one." He gestured at me.

"This isn't a democracy." General Winn growled.

Colonel Spain leaned forward in her chair. "General, we're out of ideas, unless you have one we haven't heard yet. And we are definitely out of time." She gestured at me. "This isn't the boy we thought we were recruiting, but he's what we've got. If you don't tell him, I will, and if we survive this mess, you can court-martial me."

General Winn stood. "Lieutenant?" he called through the door.

One of the soldiers waiting outside opened the door. "Yes, sir."

"Escort Colonel Spain to detention. She's to speak to no one until I say otherwise."

Colonel Spain's eyes went wide. "Are you out of your mind?"

Dr. Pierre stood. "We *need* her."

The soldier stepped close to Colonel Spain. "Ma'am, please come with me."

Colonel Spain pinched the bridge of her nose. "You're just like Eve. Do you realize that? You don't trust anyone either." She stormed out, the lieutenant close behind.

General Winn turned to me. "If you defy me one more time, you'll join her."

Dr. Pierre grunted with disgust. "This is exactly why we're in this mess. Arrogance. Yours, and the people you work with."

General Winn glared razors at him. "Would you care to join her? I can arrange that."

I didn't say anything. I had no idea what to say. I was beginning to suspect General Winn was a little out of his mind. Not downright crazy, but not completely right in the head either.

He turned back to me. "When Eve wakes up, I want you to have a heart-to-heart with her. Tell her how the soldiers stormed in and saved her life. Explain how the adults protect you, how they know better, because they've had more life experience. Tell her how you've had to get dozens of vaccinations, how when you were small you didn't understand why your mother would let people hurt you like that, but now you understand that it was for your own good, that she was protecting you from diseases much worse than the shots. Make up a story about a time you had to have surgery, and it hurt, but it saved your life. Do you understand?"

I glanced at the empty seat beside me, where Colonel Spain had been sitting. "I'll try."

"No, don't try. *Do*." He pointed at the door. "Go."

I headed for the door. There was no way I was going

to tell that made-up story about me having life-saving surgery, because Eve would sniff out the lie. But I could tell her the other stuff.

Something Colonel Spain had said in passing kept playing back in my mind: *If we survive this mess, you can court-martial me.*

If we survived *what* mess? They'd told me that many lives were at stake, but they'd never mentioned *their* lives were at stake. Just how many lives were at stake in this 'mess'? Was mine one of them?

CHAPTER 26

The soldier who'd dropped me off outside the administration building was gone, and so was my mom. I was alone. General Winn must have decided the walls around the compound and the armed soldiers in the woods beyond were enough.

I sat on a bench facing the Tulipville fountain, letting the sound of the pattering water soothe my shattered nerves. When was the last time I'd been alone, if I didn't count visits to the bathroom? It felt like ages. I missed having time to myself. Before I'd rolled into General Winn's wacko earbud school, I'd loved spending time in my room, watching videos, reading books, safe in my room.

"Benjamin!" a voice called.

I sprang from the bench. Lorena and Persephone were hurrying toward me.

"What happened?" Lorena gave me a quick clap on the shoulder to welcome me back. "Where's Eve?"

I gestured toward the perimeter field. "Let's take a walk."

As we circled the compound, I caught them up. Talking about those moments in Walmart—surrounded by police shouting orders, Eve in fully spiked meltdown mode, the soldiers storming in—it was hard to hold it together.

"Is Eve going to be okay?" Lorena asked.

"The doctors say she heals better and faster than other people, and she'll be fine in a couple of days. But it was a close call." I spotted a butterfly and couldn't help but smile, remembering Eve's encounter. The butterfly flapped in mad circles before landing on a wildflower. As it perched there, it opened and closed its wings serenely.

"We've got news too," Persephone said.

I looked up from the butterfly. "Oh really? What's that?"

"We snuck into Dr. Pierre's office yesterday." Lorena grinned. "We used the rubber doorstop trick."

I stopped walking. "Did you find out what she is?"

Persephone shook her head. "His office was filled with old books and films about experiments with monkeys."

"*Monkeys?*" I threw my hands in the air. "What does that have to do with *Eve?*"

"I did some digging," Persephone said. "Most of the material had to do with a psychologist named Harry Harlow, who took newborn baby monkeys away from their mothers and raised them in solitary confinement. Then he put each of them in a cage alone with two figures: one was made from wire and gave milk, the other was made of soft cloth and didn't."

"The wire mother, and the cloth mother," Lorena said. "We saw them in one of the videos. They were like something out of a horror movie."

"Harlow wanted to see which figure the monkeys bonded with—the one that fed them, or the one that was warm and comforting. It turned out they stayed with the cloth mother. Harlow thought that meant comfort and love was more important to the baby monkeys than food." Persephone raised her finger. "But what made Harlow famous was what happened to the baby monkeys *after*. They grew up to be monkey psychopaths. They killed their own babies as soon as they were born and attacked any monkey that tried to make friends with them. They were royally messed up."

"Sounds like Eve," I said. "She was brought up in a lab with only Adam for company, and now she's not okay. I don't say that to be mean—Eve is my friend, but let's face it, she's not okay."

"She still doesn't even know what she is," Lorena said. "That alone would screw you up. I think if she knew, it would help her."

Out beyond the perimeter fence, I caught sight of a soldier looking our way. He raised his hand in a partial wave right before he disappeared back into the foliage.

"General Winn put Colonel Spain under arrest for threatening to tell me. For some reason, he really doesn't want us to find out."

Persephone was staring at the spot where the soldier had been. "Which is a very good reason to find out. What you understand, you control; what you don't understand, controls you."

"Where is that from, anyway?" I asked. "It sounds like something Yoda would say."

"It's from my father."

That would have been my next guess. "Anyway, we've tried to find out. Twice. It's not like this is something we can Google."

Persephone and Lorena exchanged a look. "We have a plan. I pilfered and modified one of their miniature surveillance cameras. We can install it in Winn's office where we can see his keyboard. Then we steal his password and log into his account remotely."

I nearly choked. "Are you kidding me? That's—" I was going to say insane, even criminal, but how was it that different from breaking into Colonel Spain's and

General Winn's offices? "You'd still have to get inside Winn's office to install the camera, and we don't have Eve to create a diversion."

Persephone patted me on the shoulder. "That's where you come in. We need you to get General Winn to step out of his office."

"Without shutting the door," Lorena added.

I didn't like the sound of this at all.

CHAPTER 27

My heart was hammering like it wanted out of my chest as I stalked down the hall of the administration building toward General Winn's office. He was going to be furious when I said what I'd been silently rehearsing on my way over. That was the point, though. He was supposed to be furious.

His door was open. I knocked on the molding, which made my knuckles sting. Winn turned around. He raised his eyebrows. "Can I help you, Benjamin?"

"I just came to tell you I'm done. I don't care if you have my mother's permission to use me as a guinea pig. You don't have mine. I don't know what's going on, so I can't decide if this is worth risking my life over. So I'm done risking my life. Get yourself a new guinea pig."

I stalked off down the hall, counting off in my head: one Mississippi, two Mississippi, three Miss—

"Hey!" General Winn shouted.

I kept walking, knowing General Winn would follow. I needed to get him partway down the hall so he wouldn't hear Persephone slip inside his office. My insides were doing somersaults. I just was not cut out for this sort of thing.

"You're going to stop walking right now, or so help me, you're spending tonight in a cell."

I turned. "Those soldiers were going to shoot police officers if they had to. I saw them. Their fingers were on the triggers, and their safeties were off. What could be so important about Eve that US soldiers would shoot *police officers* to protect her?"

Down the hall beyond General Winn, Persephone squeezed through the door to the fire stairs. She eased it closed as quietly as possible.

"And what does that tell you?" General Winn asked.

"What do you mean?" Out of the corner of my eye, I watched Persephone slip into Winn's office.

"What does it tell you, that we're willing to go to those lengths to protect Eve?"

I didn't answer.

"I cannot risk giving you all of the details of this situation, but when I tell you the stakes literally couldn't be higher, you don't have to take my word for it. You saw for yourself just how high the stakes are."

I stammered, trying to think of something to say to keep the argument going. "I can see this means a lot to *you*. How do I know it means anything to me? Or to Eve?"

"*It's important to every single person on the planet.*" General Winn's face was beet red again. "Why am I arguing with you? Your mommy's here. Let's get her over here and you can list your grievances to her." He grabbed me by the upper arm and pulled me toward his office.

Panicked, I blurted, "I don't care if you take me back to that office and call the *president*."

General Winn stopped short. "You say that as if it's not a possibility." He rolled his eyes toward the ceiling, considering.

Behind him, Persephone scampered out of his office.

"You know what?" Winn said. "That's an even better idea. Let's call the president, and you can tell *her* you're done cooperating."

Persephone grimaced when the fire door made a clicking noise as she opened it. I coughed, trying to cover up the sound.

Winn let go of my arm. "You think I'm joking?" He curled a finger, summoning me. "Come on. I'll get her on the line."

I made a clopping sound with my tennis shoes to

mask the sound of the door closing. Of course I knew he wasn't joking about being able to call the president. I'd heard him do it.

When we reached his office, he plucked the phone receiver off its cradle.

"That's okay," I said. "I believe you."

Winn set the receiver down.

CHAPTER 28

When I got back to our dorm room, Persephone and Lorena were hunched over an old laptop.

"Guess who I almost talked to?" I asked.

Persephone looked up. "The president of the United States?"

I opened my mouth to ask how she knew, then realized they were watching Winn's office through the camera.

"He's been on the phone since you left." Lorena's eyes never left the screen. "We're waiting for him to type in his password."

Persephone pointed at the screen. "Here we go. Here we go."

General Winn hung up the phone and scooted his wheeled chair over to his computer. He typed a quick, well practice sequence on the keyboard and hit *Enter*.

Lorena pumped her fist. "Yes."

Persephone pulled up a recording of what we'd just watched and froze it at the point where Winn began typing. Zooming in for a close-up of Winn's fingers on the keyboard, she played the video in super slow-motion. Winn's fingers rose and fell as if they were underwater.

"Shift G. Small A. Shift Seven . . ." Lorena called off the keystrokes as Persephone jotted them on the back cover of her etiquette notebook. The password was a long, random string of characters. As soon as Persephone had it, she shrank the live image of General Winn and put it in the corner of the screen. She brought up General Winn's login page and typed in the password.

"Pull up his recent activity," I suggested.

Persephone typed. A list of websites scrolled down the page. Only, they weren't *.com* websites; they all ended with *.govCLASSIFIED*.

I pointed. "Looks like he's visited this one about twenty times in the last few days."

Persephone copied and pasted it onto the menu and pressed Enter.

A shock hit me like a simultaneous fist to the gut and bucket of ice water in the face.

"Oh." Lorena's voice was a whisper. "Oh."

Something with a million sides, each a different color, hung in the blackness of space. The planet Jupiter filled the left edge of the screen, its orange and grey stripes unmistakable.

"Is that a spaceship?" Persephone asked. "It's an alien ship, isn't it?"

It was huge. It was hard to tell *how* huge, because there was nothing to compare it to hanging out there in space, but you could tell it was staggeringly, awesomely enormous.

"Eve is an alien," Lorena said. "She must be."

"Everything just changed." Lorena sounded like she was in a trance. "Our entire futures, the world. Nothing will ever be the same."

Aliens. Deep down, I guess I'd believed this must be a put-on of some kind, like Persephone had suggested. "We still don't know what's going on." My lips were numb. I tried to add this new piece of the puzzle to what we already knew, but it was hard to think clearly while staring at an alien spacecraft. An actual alien spacecraft—not a *Star Wars* special effect.

Eve had been on Earth for years. The photo was date-stamped from a few months ago. Surely that spaceship hadn't been hovering out beyond Jupiter for years. Astronomers would have spotted it before now. Maybe she'd come on another ship that had visited years ago, and this was their second visit?

Persephone was exploring General Winn's files, scrolling at random. "'Updated Risk Assessment.' What's that?" She opened the file. Lorena and I stood watching over her shoulders as she read a segment aloud.

"'There is no way to predict how the Alioth will respond. It is possible they will simply schedule a new rendezvous time. However, based on our understanding of their inflexible and volatile disposition, we believe it far more likely the Alioth will react violently.'"

Lorena tapped the screen. "'How the Alioth will respond.' Respond to what?"

I had no idea.

"Wait, what's Winn saying?" Persephone expanded the screen, showing General Winn in his office, speaking on the phone.

"I don't care." Winn looked annoyed. "It doesn't matter. Your son could be Mother Teresa for all I care. We follow protocol."

I exchanged a look with Lorena and Persephone. "Your son"? Was he talking to a parent of one of the students?

"No. Too much risk." Winn shook his head, even though he was alone in the room. "You know what? I don't think this is about the mission. I think it's guilt. You feel guilty about deceiving your son. You want to alleviate that guilt. And that's about the worst reason I can imagine to make a decision that could affect every man, woman, and child on this planet, *including* Benjamin."

My vision filled with gray specks. The floor felt like it was tilting under my feet.

It was *my* mother. Winn was talking to *my* mother. Who was deceiving *me*.

"She's known all along." When we were sitting in the kitchen, talking about Eve and what she might be, Mom had known.

I headed for the door.

Persephone sprang from the bed. "Benjamin, wait. Where are you going?"

"My mother knows what's going on. She's been lying to me the whole time."

Persephone grabbed my sleeve. "She can't know that we know."

I kept walking. "She's been lying to me. My own mother has been pretending she has no idea what's going on, while the whole time she's been in on it." Why was I not surprised? The woman whose career was too important to have her son live with her for more than a few weeks a year.

"I know. But in a few hours, we'll know everything they know. Let's just lie low, figure out what's going on, and then decide what to do from there."

"I want to hear it from her." I headed out the door.

Persephone fell into step on my left, Lorena on my right.

"Benjamin, if they find out we hacked into General Winn's computer, we're going to get into huge trouble," Lorena said. "They'll throw us in juvy."

"No, they won't. Because they need us. They need something from Eve, and we're the only people Eve trusts, so they need us." We breezed past two soldiers standing outside Eve's infirmary.

Once we were inside, I looked around for Mom. She was talking to a doctor outside Eve's room. When she saw me, she smiled.

The smile faded as she took in my expression. She motioned for us to follow her into a waiting room and closed the door behind us.

"What's the matter?" Mom asked.

"You've known the whole time?" My voice was shaking with anger.

Mom gave me a look, like she had no idea what I was talking about. She opened her mouth to deny everything, then stopped. She was good at reading people. She was busted, and she knew it. "How did you find out?"

"You're a good liar, but every once in a while, there was something in your face," I said, lying. "It took me a while to figure out what it was." All this time, she knew. She *knew*. I still couldn't believe it. "What is she?"

Mom exhaled heavily, frustrated. "I can't tell you that."

I folded my arms across my chest. "Fine. Then I'm

done. When Eve wakes up, tell her I went home."

She gave me the look that meant I was in big trouble. I stood my ground.

"I'm serious," I said. "Tell us what's going on, or I'm going home, even if I have to hitchhike."

"I'm out too," Lorena put a hand on my shoulder. "We can hitch together."

Persephone lifted her hand. "Me too. Out."

Mom pulled her phone out of her back pocket, then put it back. She folded her arms, rolled her eyes up toward the ceiling, thinking. "I'm sorry I had to lie to you, I really am. I try never to lie to you as your mother, but I'm not acting as your mother in this case, I'm acting as an agent of the government. The choice isn't mine."

"Whose choice is it, then? General Winn's?" Persephone said. "The dude who put one of his own people in a cell?"

"That's right," I said. "Colonel Spain wanted to tell us. So did Dr. Pierre."

"Winn put Colonel Spain in a *cell?*" Apparently, this was news to Mom.

"He called in a lieutenant and marched her right out of his office. She told him he was out of his mind."

Mom paced the small room, hands behind her back. "You *cannot* tell Eve. Eve isn't ready to know the truth."

"All right." I looked at Persephone and Lorena. They both nodded.

"I know you know what SETI is," Mom said to me. "Lorena? Persephone? Do you know what SETI is?"

"Search for Extraterrestrial Intelligence," Persephone said. "Big satellites listening for radio transmissions from aliens."

"So Eve is an alien," I said.

"No. Eve was born on Earth." Mom swiped her hair out of her eyes. Her face was shiny with sweat. "Sixteen years ago, SETI recovered a message. A *long* message. It turned out to be a genome." Mom waited, probably for one of us to ask what a genome was. But we were the smart kids—the kids who always worked hard, the ones the teachers liked best. We all knew a genome was kind of a map of the genes that made living things what they were. And now I also knew what Eve was. They'd built her by following the genome the aliens sent, like following a recipe from a cookbook.

Unbelievable.

"SETI sent a human genome to the aliens in reply," Mom said. "That seemed to be what the aliens wanted. Then SETI created Eve and three others. This way, they could learn about the aliens."

It was hard to think about, because not only was it terrifying, but my mind kept slipping off it, thinking of it like it was a movie, or a dream, because it just couldn't be real. It was too big to be real.

"What happened to Adam?" Lorena asked.

Mom waved her hands. "That's not important right now. Stay focused."

"It is to Eve," Lorena said.

"Adam is at a different school, one just like this. But things are going even worse there than they are here." Mom held up a hand. "Just listen, okay?" Suddenly I didn't like how scared Mom looked. *All* of the adults here had that look. Underneath their grown-up, in-charge air, they were wet-your-pants terrified. "There was a second layer to the aliens' transmission that at first SETI thought was just background noise. Except, eighteen months ago, they discovered it wasn't. It was further instructions. The aliens who sent us the genome—the Alioth is what we call them—are coming. They're sending an emissary."

I exchanged a look with Lorena and Persephone. They weren't coming, they were *here*. They were hanging out near Jupiter.

"Anyone want to guess what their emissary looks like?" Mom asked.

"What?" What it *looked* like? I didn't get what she was asking.

"He looks like us." Mom waited, looking from me, to Lorena, Persephone, and back again.

He looked like us, because they'd created him from the genome we'd sent them. Which meant—

"Eve is supposed to be our emissary," Persephone whispered.

Mom nodded. "They're waiting. For Eve. Eve has to be our emissary, and if she doesn't come or they realize we didn't treat her well, we think they're going to send down an army."

"You mean, an *invasion*?" Lorena asked.

Mom didn't answer. Her expression told us everything we needed to know. I'd never been so scared. *Eve* was supposed to represent the entire human race? Eve, who flew into a rage when you looked at her wrong? Eve, who was still struggling to master the *fork*?

"We were supposed to raise Eve as one of our own." Mom dragged a hand down her sweaty face. "That's how the Alioth do this—each emissary looks like the beings they're greeting. It's a sign of respect, that you would accept this other species and raise one of their kind as your own. Only, we treated them like *lab rats*. And now we have to undo all of the damage done to Eve, and there's no time left. We have a day, maybe two before their emissary arrives."

An electric buzz of fear shot through me. *A day or two*? "Then why is she with us?" Were these people crazy? Everything depended on Eve, and they had her watching *Star Wars* and eating ice cream with thirteen-year-olds as the clock ticked down?

"They tried everything else," Mom said. "Eve is completely shut down to adults. She's with you because of an idea Dr. Pierre had. Have any of you ever heard of

Harry Harlow's monkeys?"

We exchanged a look, then all shook our heads, playing dumb.

Mom told us all the stuff we already knew, about the isolation experiments, the wire mother, and the cloth mother. I acted as if I was hearing it for the first time. Then she told us some stuff we didn't know.

"As the monkeys grew up, nothing the psychologists tried could undo the damage." Mom raised a finger. "Until they tried putting these broken adult monkeys in with *adolescent* monkeys. Somehow being with the adolescents helped them. The psychologists' best guess was the adolescent monkeys were just discovering who they were and learning how to relate to other monkeys. They could lead the broken monkeys on this journey with them and teach them how to act like monkeys."

"It worked with monkeys, so they figured it would work with an alien?" I tried to keep the sarcasm out of my tone, but it was difficult.

"It makes a weird kind of sense," Lorena said. "Eve was never going to feel better sitting around with the adults who had imprisoned and tortured her. She's still a kid, so why not try putting her with a bunch of other kids?"

I pictured Eve, all by herself, trying to figure out how to dance. She cared about what we thought of her and had even grown to like some of us. Maybe Dr. Pierre's idea wasn't that stupid.

"I wasn't part of that decision," Mom said. "I only found out about all this in August, after they picked Benjamin for the program. They needed kids whose parents worked for the government."

I made a grunting sound. "And then they gave us earbuds and told us what to say."

"They needed to steer things in the right direction and make sure you didn't say or do anything to make matters worse, or get you hurt. What if Eve overheard some of you talking about her? I don't have to tell you, kids can be mean."

I had to admit, it made more sense now that I knew what was happening.

"So the whole thing about us being handpicked for the program because of our maturity and exceptional character—that was all smoke, wasn't it?" Persephone asked.

"I think they were trying to pick reliable kids, but they were in a hurry, so I'd say it was more kids with decent grades and no disciplinary record, whose parents were willing."

"I *knew* it," Persephone said. "There was *no way* some of those kids were handpicked for their maturity."

I was more focused on the 'whose parents were willing' part, wondering again how Mom could have thrown me into this situation, knowing I had an anxiety disorder. Ever since Mom and Dad had decided it was better that I live with Dad, I'd wondered if Mom's career meant more to her than I did. That she volunteered me for this mission wasn't very reassuring.

"So now you know everything I know," Mom went on. "You have to stop making General Winn, Colonel Spain, and Dr. Pierre out to be the bad guys. We need Eve to help us, and if she hates us, she won't. You have to win her over and convince her we're all good people." Mom looked from one of us to the next. "Eve can't know what's going on yet. If she thinks the only reason we're treating her well is because we need her help, she'll shut down for good. We need to win her over, then ask for her help. Not the other way around."

"I'm not sure that's a good idea," Lorena said. "Eve likes us because we're straight with her. If we're honest with her, she'll trust us."

I could see Mom searching for the right words as she put a hand on Lorena's shoulder. "That would probably work with one of you, but Eve is an entirely different species. The psychologists on the team have spent years studying Eve, and they're convinced that if Eve finds out too soon, she'll push everyone away. More than anything, she wants her captors to pay. She wants revenge even more than she wants to be liked. That's just how her brain is wired."

There was a knock on the door. A woman's voice called, "Agent Bautista? Eve is conscious."

"You stay here," Mom said. "As soon as the doctors have checked Eve over, I'll come and get you." She paused with her hand on the doorknob. "And then I have to go face General Winn and tell him I disobeyed a direct order."

"You don't have to do that. We'll keep your secret," Persephone said. "We don't want you to lose your job over us. Right guys?"

Lorena and I agreed, but Mom waved us off. "My career is the least of our worries right now. No, the general has to know what's going on. There can't be any surprises with so much at stake."

As I watched Mom hurry off, all the strength drained out of my legs, and I had to sit down.

Persephone put a hand on my shoulder. "You okay?"

"Just give me a minute." Or a few. Better yet, give me a few years. Because the fate of Earth was suddenly resting on our shoulders—on mine, especially—and I wasn't at all ready to carry that weight.

CHAPTER 29

"A day. Maybe two." Lorena, who was leaning against a desk, looked like she might throw up. "How are we supposed to win Eve over in that amount of time? Plus, it just feels weird, being nice to her because we need something from her."

"We wanted the truth, and we finally got it," Persephone said. "Be careful what you wish for, I guess."

The door opened and Mom poked her head in. "All set, you can see Eve now."

The doctor who was treating her was waiting outside the door with Mom. "Try to get her up and walking," the doctor said. "That would be the best thing for her now."

As I watched Eve through the glass wall, it was

hard not to look at her differently. She'd gone from being a monster out of my nightmares, to a strange and unpredictable kid who I felt very sorry for, to the only person on Earth who could save us from an alien invasion. No wonder they'd freaked out when I smuggled her to a Walmart. I never would have done it if I'd known.

We filed quietly into the room. Eve was sitting up in her cocoon, a cup of light blue liquid on the table beside her. She was wearing her butterfly earrings.

"How are you feeling?" I asked.

"They shot me."

"I saw. They shot you with electricity."

"The doctors say you healed fast, though." Lorena was leaning up against the glass wall, her arms tucked behind her back, looking uncomfortable. "Much faster than we would."

"Because I'm not like you. Because I'm different."

I felt a rising panic. We didn't want to go there; we didn't want to talk about how she was different. Not yet.

"I love your earrings," Persephone said. "Butterflies. They're perfect."

"It's your spirit animal," Lorena added. "Each of us has a spirit animal that represents—"

"Did they tell you what I am?" Eve asked.

"No," I said, a little too quickly. "But I got in huge trouble for sneaking you out. No Xboxes for me until I'm, like, sixty." The lie felt like a brick lodged in my gut.

We were the only three people in the world Eve trusted, and we were lying to her. I could see from their faces that Lorena and Persephone were as miserable as I was.

An awkward silence stretched.

"I just love those earrings," Lorena finally said.

Eve was studying me, or listening to me, or whatever she did with those things on her face. "What happens now? Am I going back to the lab?"

"Of course not," I said.

"We would never let that happen," Persephone said.

"We care about you," Lorena added.

Eve was studying Lorena now, moving her head from side to side, and up and down, like she was looking for something. Her lie detector was going off, and she was trying to locate the source.

"So you haven't found out what I am?" she asked.

Persephone shook her head. "We're trying our hardest."

Eve went very still. Her barbs *flexed*, just barely brushing the surface of her skin.

This felt like a mistake. If you needed someone's help, you *asked* them, you didn't manipulate them into helping you. I couldn't understand how Winn and Dr. Pierre, and even my own mother, didn't see that. I wanted to help them—to help *us*. Maybe the only way to help them was to do the opposite of what they'd told me to do.

"Why don't we take a walk?" I gave Persephone and Lorena a look. *Help me out here.* I motioned toward the door. "Come on, Eve. The doctor said it would be good for you."

Eve didn't budge.

"Yeah, it's nice out," Lorena said. "Come on, Eve."

Reluctantly, Eve rolled off the bed. She followed us out, head down.

My heart was pounding like a jackhammer as we marched out into the field, away from cameras and microphones. Now that we were out here, I was having serious second thoughts about this. What if I was wrong? What if telling Eve the truth really did ruin any chance we had of getting her to cooperate?

She *knew* we were lying, though. It was so obvious—at this very moment, she was concluding that she couldn't trust us either, that she couldn't trust anyone, that she was on her own. We couldn't reach her if she didn't trust us, and she would never trust us if we lied to her, because she could taste those lies as soon as they were out of our mouths.

"Eve." I was going to have a heart attack. At thirteen years old, I was going to drop dead of a coronary. "The reason everyone is being so nice to you—"

Persephone slowed slightly and caught my eye behind Eve's back. She shook her head, her eyes wide in alarm.

". . . is because they need you to save the world, but

they're afraid you won't do it, because they treated you so badly."

Eve's barbs came bursting out. It occurred to me that her barbs were like my racing heart.

"Did they tell you what I am?" she asked.

"*Benjamin*—" Persephone said.

"Yes," I said.

"Tell me." Eve's voice was quiet, maybe scared. Maybe terrified.

Persephone shook her head, warning me, but she didn't utter a word to try to stop me, which was smart, because I think Eve would have filleted anyone who tried to silence me at that moment.

I doubted they'd taught Eve anything about genetics. I took a deep breath and tried to explain it. "You're sort of from another planet. You were born on Earth, but aliens sent instructions to Earth for how to make someone who looks like them. That's you. The government followed the instructions the aliens sent, and made you."

Eve was trembling all over. Her barbs sank back into her skin until her skin puckered. Then the barbs erupted all over again.

"It's a lot to take in, I know," I said.

"I'm . . . an alien." Eve sounded surprised, but not necessarily upset. "Like Chewbacca."

"Exactly." Why hadn't I thought of that?

"Technically, you're an Alioth-American," Persephone

said. "That's the name of the alien species—Alioth. You're Alioth, but since you were born in the United States, you're also an American citizen."

"You're also a miracle," Lorena said. "You're very special, and very important."

"Because I'm supposed to save the world." Eve continued walking. "How?"

"You're supposed to be our emissary," I said. "It's the only way the Alioth will meet with us. General Winn and his people were supposed to raise you for that purpose, but they screwed everything up."

"I won't help them," Eve said.

Persephone and I exchanged an alarmed glance.

"Eve, they're going to *invade* if you don't," Persephone said. "They'll kill us all. Not just General Winn. *Everyone.* Me, Lorena, Benjamin. Maybe even you."

"I'm glad they need my help, so I can say no. They never let us go outside. We never got to do *anything* except be hurt. For years and years. They hurt Adam more than they hurt me." Eve stopped walking. "Did they tell you where Adam is?"

"He's at another school, just like this one." *But things are going even worse there*, Mom had said. Maybe they were trying to convince him to be the emissary as well. That was slightly reassuring—if we failed with Eve, there might still be a chance.

"Wait," Lorena said. "What if we got them to agree

to bring Adam here, if you promise to help us?" It was a brilliant idea. I held my breath, waiting.

"How about it, Eve?" Persephone prodded. "Isn't that a great idea?"

Eve shook her head. "They'd just take him away after I did what they wanted."

"I don't think this is a one-time thing," I said. "The Alioth are here. They're not going to turn around and go home any time soon." At least, I didn't think they were. "General Winn is going to need your help for a long time. We all are."

Persephone put a hand on Eve's shoulder, careful to place it where there were no barbs. "You'll have the power, Eve. Just like you have it right now. You have all the power. They're desperate—they'll do anything to get you to say yes." She gestured toward the top of The Cyclone's twisty red track, poking up over the school. "They built you an amusement park, they flew across an entire state to bring you food. If you say yes, you'll have all the power."

Persephone's knees were visibly shaking. I could hear my heart beating in my ears. We all watched Eve, trying to read her inscrutable face, holding our breath.

"If they bring Adam here, and Adam gets to live with us at Benjamin's house, and Persephone and Lorena move in next door and across the street, I'll do it."

We broke into a cheer. I pumped my fist in the air.

Lorena let out a delighted laugh. "My mom is going to *freak* when they tell her we're moving."

"Let's go tell General Winn." Persephone took off at a jog toward the compound.

Lorena and I went to follow, but Eve didn't budge.

"What's the matter?" I asked.

"I don't want to speak to him. I don't want to see him."

And it was probably a bad idea if she did. The sight of him might make Eve change her mind. "Why don't you wait here and look for butterflies while we talk to them? We'll come get you once it's all worked out."

We ran for the compound. I felt lighter than I'd been in weeks. In *years*. We'd done it. We'd saved the whole freaking world. I had no doubt they'd pull Adam from his school in an eye blink once they heard Eve was willing to be the emissary. She was the one they really seemed to want, after all.

We ran through Star Wars Park, across the access road, up the steps and right past the guard stationed outside the administration building.

"Hey! Hold it!" she shouted.

Giggling, we ignored her and headed down the long hallway.

I could hear my mother's voice drifting through General Winn's open door. We piled in without knocking.

Gasping for breath, I said, "We got Eve to agree to

do it. All she wants is for you to bring Adam here and let him live with us after it's over."

"And me and Persephone have to move in next door," Lorena added. "That's part of the agreement."

General Winn's eye flew wide. Mom's mouth dropped open.

"What?" I said, looking from Mom to General Winn and back again, confused. "She wants a few stupid little things in exchange for saving the world."

"You told her?" Mom looked livid and very, very scared. "The one thing we told you not to do, you did?"

General Winn shook his head in disbelief. "You stupid ignorant brats. What have you done?"

"We got you what you wanted, that's what we did." I licked my extremely dry lips. "Didn't we?"

Mom's face was buried in her hands.

General Winn sprang to his feet, nearly knocking his chair over. He grabbed my arm. "Let's go. You can tell them yourself." He tugged me out of his office, squeezing my arm so hard I yelped in pain.

"Let go of him right now," Mom said. "I don't care what he did. Let him go, or I'll tear that hand off at the wrist."

General Winn let go of my arm. "Come on. All of you, follow me."

He led us down the hall, turned right into the smaller hall. He stopped at one of the doorways where we'd hidden a few days before. I looked at Mom, trying to understand what was going on, what we'd done wrong. She wouldn't even meet my eyes. Persephone and Lorena looked flat-out terrified.

The door slid open. I'd been expecting a room and was surprised to find it was an elevator. We followed General Winn inside. There were only two buttons—*Top*, and *Bottom*.

We headed down in silence. The ride was longer than I would have guessed—we were going way below ground. It gave me a lot of time to marinate in my fear, to wonder why what seemed like such an obvious slam-dunk easy deal with Eve was such a problem.

The door finally opened onto a round, theater-sized room that reminded me of the NASA control room— dozens of people sat at consoles, others rushed around or stood talking in small groups. Over their shoulders, I could see that many of the screens were connected to the surveillance cameras all over the campus. One of these people was probably Earbud Guy.

"Madam President," General Winn called. He turned to me and barked, "Follow me."

Madam President? I scanned the faces until I spotted her, six inches taller than the people around her, built like a football player or a pro wrestler. Elsa Cauthen, the president of the United States. Suddenly I needed to go to the bathroom.

"We have a new problem," Winn said as we

approached her. The others who'd been standing with her melted away.

President Cauthen gestured toward an open door. "Let's talk in here." She called five or six names, and people peeled off from what they were doing and headed for the door. I glanced back at Mom, Persephone, and Lorena to make sure they were following as well.

It was a conference room with a long cherrywood table and black chairs on wheels. General Winn gestured for me to sit next to him. When everyone had found a seat, he was the first to speak.

"Our genius children have leaked the end game to Eve. They promised her a reunion with Adam in exchange for her cooperation."

The president pressed her palm across her forehead, as if she'd just developed a migraine. "Does she know everything? What she is? All of it?"

General Winn looked pointedly at me.

"Yes, ma'am." My voice warbled and shook and was barely audible.

"We need to pull her out of there and go with established influence techniques. Solitary confinement, sleep deprivation," a grizzled old guy with a handlebar mustache said. "This was an awful idea from the start."

"You can't punish someone into representing you." Hearing my mom speak startled me. "The Alioth will find out."

"Just let her see Adam. Why can't you bring him here?" It just came out. I didn't even know I was going to speak until my mouth was moving. I think I was in shock—it was like I was standing outside myself, watching.

"That's not an option," General Winn snarled at me. "Drop it."

"We need to go back to the earbuds," a woman with wild, curly hair said. "We'll camouflage them better this time, then send the kids back to Eve, and we negotiate through them. Give her anything she wants—to live at Disney World, to ride the rides with all of the *Star Wars* actors, to *star* in the next *Star Wars* film—"

"She wants *Adam*," Lorena shouted over her. "She's not three, she's thirteen. Why can't you just let her see Adam?"

"Because Adam is dead," Persephone said.

The room fell silent.

I turned to Persephone, stunned. "How do you know that?"

"Adam wasn't in any of the later videos from the lab. Plus, it's the only logical explanation for why they won't let Eve see him. They won't, because they can't."

I looked at my mom. "There's no second school? That was another lie?"

Mom didn't answer. She wouldn't look at me. I turned toward the president.

President Cauthen nodded. "Adam is dead. If Eve finds out, all hope is lost. That's why we had to lie to you. One of the reasons."

"Except by lying to us, we didn't know not to promise Eve that she can see him," Persephone said.

"*You weren't supposed to promise her anything.*" General Winn pounded his fist on the table.

"I did that, not Persephone," I said. "Persephone tried to stop me."

"None of this is helpful." The president looked different than she did on TV. Older, sweatier. Like it had been days since she'd showered. "We are out of time, and we need a plan. Stop pointing fingers, and start making suggestions."

"Earbuds. Promise her anything," the woman with the wild hair said.

"You still don't get her. You studied her for years, and you still don't get her at all," I muttered.

"What do you suggest, Benjamin?" General Winn asked. "There's no Adam to bring to her. What do you suggest we do?"

"I don't know. But not earbuds and promises."

The room fell silent. I swallowed. I needed a drink of water worse than I ever had in my life.

"Take her back to Benjamin's house, where she's happiest," Lorena said. "Let Persephone and me go too. We'll watch movies and eat pizza and try to convince Eve that this world is worth saving."

I pointed at Lorena. "That's a good idea."

General Winn scowled at me. "Coming from the person who backed us into this corner in the first place, I'm not sure that's a ringing endorsement."

"Coming from the guy who thought it was a good idea to treat our emissary like a lab rat for thirteen years, I'm not sure you're the right person to be talking about who backed us into a corner," I shot back.

My mother covered her mouth to stifle a laugh, which surprised the heck out of me. I'd expected her to chew me out for being disrespectful to an adult.

"Did neither of you hear me when I said no more finger-pointing?" President Cauthen stared razors at me. I looked down at my hands.

"Other suggestions?" President Cauthen looked around the table. "That's it? Our options are solitary confinement, earbuds and promises, and a pizza party? The top strategists and scientists this country has to offer are stifled by one adolescent alien?"

General Winn started to say something, but President Cauthen silenced him with a warning glance. "I've heard enough from you." She locked her intimidating gaze on me. "I can't believe I'm saying this, but given the options, I'm inclined to go with the pizza party. These three kids are the only people who've managed to get Eve to like them." President Cauthen raised a finger in warning. "Do not, under any circumstances, tell her about Adam," The president looked from me, to Lorena, to Persephone. "Understand?"

I nodded. "Yes, ma'am."

"If you need something, just ask."

We needed a miracle, I wanted to say. Instead, I said, "Yes, ma'am."

The president stood. Everyone else jumped up. She looked from me, to Lorena, to Persephone. "I'm sorry to lay this burden on you. Maybe Eve is right. Maybe we don't deserve her help. Somehow we have to convince her to help us anyway. Somehow *you* have to convince her."

CHAPTER 30

As soon as Eve spotted us coming across the quad, she broke into a stiff-legged run.

"When can I see Adam? You'll like him. We can all be friends and have movie nights together." The hope in Eve's voice felt like daggers through my heart. Poor Eve.

I swallowed and delivered the lie we'd agreed on. "They said Adam needs to stay at his school until this is over."

Eve's spines bulged.

I took a half step back, afraid she would lash out at me, and quickly added, "But they agreed to everything else."

A low hiss boiled up from deep inside Eve. "I have

the power. If they won't bring Adam, I won't help them."

We'd agreed not to try to talk Eve into anything until we were at my house and Eve was in a good mood.

"Guess what?" Lorena said. "We're all going to Benjamin's house. It's going to be *awesome*. We're going to have a nonstop party."

Eve huffed and folded her arms across her barrel chest. "They won't change my mind by being nice to me."

I heard the *thump-thump* of a helicopter, growing louder.

"It was Lorena's idea, actually. Not theirs." Persephone said.

The army green helicopter appeared, flying low over the treetops.

Persephone pointed. "Here comes our ride now. So, what movie should we watch first when we get there?"

Eve didn't answer.

CHAPTER 31

Eve lifted a slice of pizza from the box, took a halfhearted bite, and dropped it back into the box. Even she could only eat so much.

Lorena was standing by the stairwell, talking to her mother on the phone, her finger plugging her free ear.

"You should have heard the president at that meeting," Persephone said, watching Eve out of the corner of her eye. "Every time General Winn tried to open his mouth, she told him to shut up. She's so angry at him for how he treated you."

Eve reached for the popcorn. She didn't seem to be listening to Persephone.

I thumbed through the movie options on the TV,

looking for something Eve would like. Something that would give us all a lift.

My heart had been pounding nonstop since we took off from Sagantown. I was sick with fear, and Lorena and Persephone looked like they were as well. It was hard to act lighthearted and fun when you were less than twenty-four hours from Armageddon.

"Okay, Mom. I heard you," Lorena said into the phone. "I have to go. I love you too." She hung up and tossed her phone onto the couch beside her. "What are we watching? Or maybe we should put on some music?"

Eve studied the phone lying on the cushion. "Can I talk to Adam on that?"

"No," Persephone and I said simultaneously.

Eve picked up the phone, turned it over in her hands. "Why not?"

"There are no phones allowed at the schools," Persephone said. "Remember? None of us were allowed to have one."

Eve made a puffing sound. "They built a whole school for me. They built a roller coaster, an ice cream shop. All I want is to see Adam, and they say no. It makes no sense."

No, it didn't make any sense whatsoever. I couldn't think of any scenario where it would make sense if Adam was alive.

"I'm worried about him." Eve turned to me. "Can't

you ask your mom again? She must know."

"I've asked her so many times. She's not important enough. There are a lot of things they don't tell her."

Eve studied me carefully. "Are you lying to me?"

"No." My voice came out an octave too high. I was a bad liar. Part of it was I didn't have much practice, but even with practice I doubted I'd ever be very good at it.

Lorena started to speak, then stopped. She looked at me.

My mother once told me whenever you're in doubt about whether to lie or tell the truth, go with the truth. Sometimes you *have* to lie, like when your friend asks if you like his new haircut, and it's horrible. This didn't feel like one of those times. Eve had been lied to, imprisoned, experimented on, treated like one of Harlow's monkeys. Yet President Cauthen had told us it definitely *was* one of those times.

I wiped a tear from under my eye. I was so tired, so scared. I didn't know what the right thing to do was anymore.

Seeing that tear uncorked something in Lorena, and she started to cry silent tears as well. She wiped her cheeks with her sleeve, but fresh tears kept coming. I wasn't sure if we were crying for Eve, or Adam, or ourselves.

Eve was watching us carefully. "Why are you crying? I don't understand."

"I don't either." Persephone looked terribly confused.

Lorena was still looking right at me. She wanted to tell Eve the truth. This final, terrible lie felt wrong to her. It felt wrong to me too.

I nodded to her, ever so slightly.

Lorena squinted at me. *Are we sure?* Her eyes asked.

No, I wasn't. But we only had a few hours left, and this wasn't working. We had to do something different. So far, telling Eve the truth hadn't helped at all, just as Mr. Pierre's people had predicted. But my heart told me this was the right thing to do, and Lorena's eyes told me hers did too.

I nodded again. Lorena nodded back. She turned to Persephone.

"We've got to tell her, Perse."

"Tell me what?" Eve asked.

Persephone squeezed her eyes closed and pressed the heels of her palms to her temples. I was sure she was going to argue or scream for the soldiers, but instead, eyes still closed, she nodded.

Lorena turned to Eve, and in a soft voice, said, "Adam's gone, Eve. He's dead. I'm so sorry."

Eve's barbs turned inward, covering her with little divots. "They killed Adam?" She stayed very still for a moment. "They lied." She pointed at me. "*You* lied." She pointed at Lorena. "You lied." And then Persephone, who was shaking her head slowly, her face buried in her hands. "You lied."

"They said you'd never help if we told you the truth," I said.

"They were right."

"But we're going to die," Lorena said. "Doesn't that mean anything to you?"

"You're all liars. You deserve to die." Eve's tone was ice cold and rock hard.

Lorena stared her down. "No one deserves to die, even if they make mistakes."

Without moving a muscle, except the ones that worked her wide mouth, Eve said, "Go away."

"We *can't*," I said. "There's no more time." When Eve didn't answer, I clasped my hands together like I was praying. Or begging. "We're not all bad. My grandpa has long hair and dances to heavy metal music. You can meet him when this is over. I can't wait for that time, when you're my sister, and we're all living on the same street."

Eve twisted, turning her back to me. "You're saying that because you need me."

"Heck yes, I need you. But I'm not saying it because I need you. You're a friend. You're *becoming* a friend, anyway, and when someone's your friend you—"

"*Adam* was my friend."

My shoulder was suddenly on fire. Blood poured down my sleeve. I hadn't even seen Eve move.

"I loved him, and they killed him. I wouldn't help them for anything. Not for anything." She glanced up and seemed surprised we were still there. "Go away, or I'll do much worse."

Persephone and Lorena grabbed me by the elbows and half carried me toward the stairs. Behind us, there was a squealing, crunching sound as Eve ripped the TV off the wall.

She raised it over her head and hurled it at us. I ducked as it hit the handrail and ricocheted over me, catching Persephone on the side of the head. Persephone fell backward, tumbled down the steps, and landed hard, facedown on the concrete floor.

Lorena and I rushed down to her. I grabbed Persephone's arms, Lorena grabbed her legs, and we carried her up the steps as, behind us, Eve ransacked the room.

The door flew open just before we reached it. Mom took one look at us and shouted for the doctor.

CHAPTER 32

I barely felt the sting of the needle as the doctor gave me a shot to numb my shoulder.

Mom patted my good shoulder. "It's not too bad." She thought I was upset and shaking because of the cut.

"I don't care about the cut." The burning in my shoulder barely registered. Deep down, I'd truly believed Eve cared about us more than she hated General Winn. I was wrong. Nothing was bigger than her hate.

"How is Persephone?" They'd taken her to another room.

"She'll be fine. No concussion, just bruised."

The doctor getting ready to stitch my arm pressed his free hand on my wrist. "Hold still." I took a deep breath and tried to stop twitching and shaking. As the doctor began the first stitch, I could hear the thread sliding through my skin, but I couldn't feel it.

"You told her, didn't you?" Mom asked.

I couldn't get my mouth to form the word *yes*, so instead I asked, "What happens now?"

"Someone will go in Eve's place. They'll tell the Alioth Eve is sick. The Alioth were *very* clear about the terms of the meeting, but it's a chance."

I kept my face turned so I couldn't see the wound or the stitching. There was a tray of fresh-baked brownies sitting on the kitchen table beside me. More bribes for Eve. It was too late for bribes.

Another *crash* in the basement. Eve had found something else to smash.

"What happens to Eve?" I asked.

Mom sighed heavily. "I imagine they'll take her back to the lab. Or put her in a cell and leave her there until this is over, one way or another."

Mostly, I felt bad about that. Mostly. She'd attacked us. We'd been nothing but nice to her, and she'd attacked us. And now, who knew what was going to happen?

"Try to hold still," the doctor urged me. I was trying, but I couldn't stop shaking.

CHAPTER 33

The helicopter that would take Eve away set down in the front yard, kicking up dust and spraying debris that ticked and clattered against the kitchen window. General Winn's crew-cut head poked out of the cockpit, filling me with rage and a crawling feeling of disgust. Winn jumped to the ground and headed toward the house.

Maria opened the front door from outside, then stepped aside as General Winn stormed in. He glanced at me, eyes blazing with rage, then looked away. I joined Lorena, Persephone, and Mom in the living room.

"*I don't want to go.*" Eve's voice reached us from the basement. "*I'll hurt you.*"

One of the soldiers down there was shouting directions

to the others. "Get around her. *Watch it, watch it.*"

The wound on my shoulder throbbed. The numbing shot was wearing off.

The door flew open, and three soldiers dragged Eve from the basement. They were holding the ends of poles about four feet long that had sleeves on the end. Two of the sleeves were tight around Eve's wrists; the third was wrapped around her neck. Her barbs were fully extended.

"I want to stay," Eve wailed. "I want to stay here with Benjamin and Lorena and Persephone and watch *Star Wars*." Eve spotted us as they led her toward the front door. "I'm sorry, Benjamin. I'm sorry, Persephone."

I turned away. I couldn't watch.

"I'm sorry," she called as they led her away. There was such sorrow in her voice. In a lot of ways she was like a toddler, the way her emotions swung from one extreme to another so quickly. I imagined her sitting in an empty cell, her arms wrapped around her head like one of Harlow's monkeys, alone, no friends, no family. It was messed up that she refused to help us, but it wasn't her fault she was messed up.

Lorena was crying quietly. Persephone was close to tears.

Eve's strangled voice drifted from the front of the house. "I'm sorry."

"I can't stand it." I sprang from my chair and bounded down the hall.

"Benjamin!" Mom called after me.

I raced out the front door. "Leave her alone!" I ran ahead and blocked the lead soldier's path to the helicopter. He shoved me aside, almost knocking me down.

Hands grasped my arm, helping me up. It was Persephone.

"Let her go," Lorena shouted at the soldiers. "You've hurt her enough."

Persephone and I raced to get in front of the soldier again. When he tried to push us aside, we stood our ground. He shifted direction, trying to get around us.

"Benjamin?" Eve's barbs were gone.

I slipped past the soldier and wrapped my arms around Eve. I pulled against the force of the soldiers, back toward the house.

"Are you nuts?" one of the soldiers shouted. "She'll cut you to shreds."

General Winn appeared, waving his arms violently. "Benjamin! Get out of there."

A hand grasped my wrist. It was Lorena, wrapping her arms around Eve's big body. Persephone took my other hand. A soldier grabbed me by the waist and tried to pull me away. I held tight to Persephone and Lorena.

"Let go of him," Mom shouted. She turned to General Winn. "*Enough.*"

"She's too dangerous to have wandering around loose. Haven't you figured that out by now?" General

Winn shouted.

"I'll take responsibility, for all that matters at this point. Just, *go*." Mom pointed at the helicopter.

Winn opened his mouth to say something, probably to argue some more. His squared shoulders slumped ever so slightly. He headed for the helicopter.

Mom pushed past the soldiers and grasped the cuff on Eve's left hand. "Get these things off of her." I got to work on the right one as the soldiers backed off. They seemed confused about what to do and who was in charge.

"I'm sorry I hurt you, Benjamin," Eve said as Persephone worked on the sleeve wrapped around her neck.

When we had the cuffs off, Mom placed her hands on Eve's shoulders and looked her straight in the ear-eyes. "I know it was hard to hear about Adam. I know you're angry. But I need your promise that you won't hurt anyone again."

"I promise. I won't hurt anyone. Not even General Winn." Little points like thorns sprouted from Eve's plum-colored skin, and her voice got low and hard. "But I won't help him."

She was sorry, but not sorry enough to save our lives. I almost said it out loud, but I was afraid she might go back on her word and give me another gash.

We filed into the house in dead silence.

"I want to watch movies and eat pizza." Eve looked exhausted. There were yellowish welts where the sleeves had been wrapped on her wrists.

"Come on," I said, "we can watch in my bedroom." Because, you know, you wrecked the basement.

We crowded into my bedroom—Eve on the bed; me, Persephone, and Lorena a safe distance away on the floor. I put on *Teen Titans Go! To the Movies*. It was funny, but no one laughed. I couldn't stop thinking about Alioth warships filling the skies. My stomach was in knots. Persephone and Lorena seemed to be staring right through the TV screen. Tears were flowing silently down Lorena's cheeks.

She noticed me looking at her and tried to give me an encouraging smile, but it collapsed as she wiped the tears with her sleeve.

From up on the bed, Eve whispered, "Adam."

"They're not going to let you stay here," I said, since no one seemed to be watching the movie anyway. "Whatever happens out there, they're going to come and put you in a cell."

"I'm still not going to be the emissary."

"I know." I raised up until I could see Eve. "We get it. You can stop saying it." I dropped back to the floor and watched the Teen Titans battle Balloon Man. I'd seen the movie about five times, but I still couldn't follow the plot in the mental state I was in. It was hard to imagine that outside the fence surrounding our property, everyone was going about their lives, clueless to what was happening. Meanwhile, my stomach was lurching so badly I thought I might throw up.

We'd blown it. They'd told us not to tell Eve about Adam, and we'd told her anyway. They'd warned us this was what would happen.

"Then why did you help me?" Eve asked.

I lifted up again. "What do you mean?"

"If you know I'm not going to be the emissary, why did you stop them from taking me?"

Lorena sat up. "Because we care about you, Eve. We couldn't stand to see you suffer like that. We're really angry at you, and disappointed, and terrified, but we still care about you."

Eve returned her gaze to the screen. She tilted her big head, like she was trying to understand what was happening. But I think she was trying to understand what Lorena had just said. She was trying to understand compassion. She didn't get the whole idea of caring what happened to someone even if you didn't want something from them. And how could she? No one had ever shown her compassion. No one had ever been nice to her until they needed something from her.

There was a *bang* outside. I jolted, my heart suddenly racing.

"Probably just a truck or something," Persephone

said. "I think we'll know if it starts."

We went back to pretending to watch the movie. This waiting, the not knowing, was torture.

"I would say the wrong thing anyway," Eve said. "I would make things worse."

We all turned. Was she saying what I thought she was saying? I felt like I must have misheard her, because this was a completely different reason for not wanting to be the emissary.

"You have a good heart," Lorena said. "They'd see that. They'd like you, just like we do."

Eve shook her head. "I would say the wrong things. They would laugh at me."

Suddenly a lot of things fell into place. She was scared. Eve was just figuring out how to talk to other people, how to eat with a fork, how to be a friend, and suddenly people were asking her to be the world's emissary, to speak to the representative of an alien race. It was like someone handing me a scalpel and saying, *Here. Go perform brain surgery on the president.*

It wasn't that her hate for General Winn was stronger than her love for us. She was just a kid, and she was scared to death. Hating General Winn was just an excuse.

I tried to think of something to say that would make her less afraid. If I was in her shoes, what would make me feel less scared?

I looked at Persephone, then at Lorena. They

looked back at me, wide-eyed. They'd come to the same realization.

I tried to think, but it was hard, knowing we were out of time. What would make me feel less afraid if I had to meet with aliens with the weight of the world on my shoulders?

Think of something. Think. I stared at my friends. They stared back at me.

My friends. Knowing my friends had my back made me less afraid. Having someone to share the weight with me.

I took a breath to slow my racing heart, desperately not wanting to suggest what I was about to suggest. "What if I went with you?"

I watched Eve, trying to read her wide, unreadable alien face. She lifted her half eaten slice of pizza and took a bite, chewing slowly. "They would let you?"

"You have the power. If you say you'll only do it if I come with you, then I come with you." As an afterthought, I added, "Heck, I bet it would be fun." It would not be fun. Walking into an alien spacecraft would not be fun. But I needed to sell this. Eve seemed to be considering.

"You're my friends, and I care about you," Eve said.

All three of us leaned toward Eve.

"Are you saying yes?" Persephone asked.

Eve chewed. I was almost afraid to breathe.

"Only for you. And for Benjamin's mother."

I looked at Eve, a numb warmth rushing through my limbs, my vision going spotty. In my mind I saw Eve as she'd looked the very first time, sitting in that classroom like a nightmare come to life. Then I saw her riding her motorcycle around the hall, and trying to figure out how to dance, and throwing tubs of ice cream, and meeting a butterfly. We'd been through so much together.

We'd felt sure the adults had Eve wrong, that she wasn't the self-centered psychopath they thought she was, just a traumatized, terrified kid with a good heart. And we'd been right.

I looked up at Lorena and Persephone: they were hugging each other and crying. I realized I was crying too.

We'd done it. We'd really done it.

I sprang from the floor. "Thank you. Thank you so much." Saying thank you didn't seem like enough, though. "Can I hug you?"

Eve climbed off the couch. "All right." She sounded pleased. Excited, almost.

"Those spikes won't pop out if I do, will they?"

"I promised."

I took a step toward her. "Okay, then." I wrapped my arms around her wide middle. She felt sort of mushy and smelled like mud. I hadn't noticed that the last time I was this close to her, because there was too much else going on at the time. The pucker spots appeared, her spikes turning inward. She pressed her strange arms to my back.

Lorena was waiting for her turn as I let go.

"Thank you, Eve," she whispered, and kissed Eve on the cheek.

"I have to go tell Mom." I ran into the hall, past a soldier, and down the stairs so fast I lost my footing and slid down the last few.

Mom was in the kitchen, drinking tea, looking miserable.

"You have to call the president," I sputtered. "She's gonna do it."

Mom sprang up. "*What*? Are you sure?"

"She said she'll do it if I go with her."

Mom knocked her chair over as she bounded from the kitchen, shouting, "Get the president on the line. I need to speak to the president *now*."

I ran back upstairs.

"What does an emissary wear?" Eve was asking Lorena and Persephone.

"Anything she wants, I imagine," Persephone said.

"I'd go with your blue dress," Lorena said. "Blue signifies peace and love. Unless you want to go with purple, which is a mixture of blue and the fierce energy of red. Yes, maybe purple."

"Just, pick fast," I said. "We have to get going. The Alioth are waiting."

CHAPTER 34

President Cauthen looked across our kitchen table at Eve, who was chewing on a slice of brownie the size of a dinner plate. "Is there anything else you need?"

"Yes," Eve said without hesitation.

President Cauthen waited. Finally, she asked, "What is it?"

Eve pointed at General Winn. "I never want to see him again. I want Benjamin's mom in charge. I want her to be president."

President Cauthen smiled. "Well, she can't be president, because that's my job." She eyed General Winn. "But I'm willing to put her in charge of this operation. Is that acceptable, Emissary Eve?"

Eve looked at me.

I nodded.

"Yes," Eve said.

President Cauthen turned to General Winn. "As of now, you're relieved of duty. Agent Bautista, you're in charge of the Alioth operation. You answer to no one but me."

"Yes, Madam President." Mom looked stunned. I'm sure the thought of having the fate of the world on her shoulders terrified her. I knew how she felt. Mom could handle it, though. She was a rock.

General Winn took off his hat festooned with shiny brass. He looked like he might throw up. His lab rat had just gotten him fired. Without looking at anyone, he turned and headed for the door.

I almost felt sorry for him. Almost.

President Cauthen raised her chin. "Anything else?"

Once again, Eve looked at me. I tried to think of anything else Eve should ask for, while she had all the power in the world.

"The students from our middle school deserve to be at the rendezvous point to see how it ends," I said. "They all helped."

Eve looked at President Cauthen. "I want all the students to be there."

President Cauthen sighed heavily. "That's going to complicate things, but okay." She turned to an aide.

"Arrange to have the students flown to the rendezvous point immediately."

The aide rushed out of the room.

President Cauthen pressed her palms to the desk, poised to stand. "Are we good?"

Eve waited for me.

"I think you're good," I said.

"I'm good," Eve repeated.

The president stood. "Then it's your rodeo, Agent Bautista. Make it happen."

Mom put one hand on Eve's shoulder, the other on mine. "Major Martinez, get the blades turning on the chopper. I want Emissary Eve and her assistant in the air in three minutes."

"Yes, ma'am." A woman wearing slightly less shiny brass than General Winn took off at a sprint, shouting orders.

"That was a nice call, firing General Winn," I said to Eve.

"I have the power." Eve said.

I grinned at Eve. "You have the power."

We hurried outside into blinding sunlight. The chopper was waiting on the lawn, engine running. It was bigger than the one we'd used before. We climbed a steel ramp into a big, dimly lit space in the back of the chopper. I took a bucket seat along the wall and pressed my palms to my knees, trying to calm my legs. They wouldn't stop shaking.

Lorena and Persephone vaulted up the ramp.

"Eve." Lorena beckoned with a wave of her hand, pointing to the seats across from me. "Come sit by us." That was a great idea. Lorena was good at calming people, and Eve definitely needed calming.

Mom took the seat beside me.

The chopper rose straight up, then quickly surged forward, just clearing the treetops beyond the fence.

"None of us has the right to put this weight on your shoulders," Mom said to me. "Least of all me. I've always believed my job was so important, that so many lives were at stake, that I had to put it first. I'm so sorry. From now on, you always come first. And just know I'm so proud of you I could bust."

I was too choked up to speak, so I gave her a hug and left it at that.

Mom's eyes were filled with tears. "You've grown up." She snapped her fingers. "Two months ago, you were a kid, and now you're not."

"I figure I'm going to start seeing gray hairs before much longer."

Laughing, Mom rubbed the top of my head. Then she pulled out a comb and fixed my hair. Which made sense. When you were going to meet the emissary of an alien race, you should probably try to look your best. "Why me? Why did they sit me right next to Eve in that classroom? Weren't they afraid I'd have a panic attack and blow it?"

"They put you there *because* of your anxiety, or at least partly because of it," Mom said. "They thought Eve might relate to you because, like she said at Thanksgiving, she's terrified all the time."

I noticed Eve, Lorena, and Persephone looking my way. "I'd better check on Eve." I unbuckled my seatbelt and went over to join them.

"We were just telling Eve what each of us thought she was, back when we first met her." Persephone shook her head. "We were all wrong."

"I was kind of close," I said.

"So was I," Lorena said.

Persephone gawked at her. "You thought she was a magical being, and she turned out to be an extraterrestrial American. How were you close?"

"She can be both."

Persephone rolled her eyes.

"We're all simultaneously different things on different planes of existence," Lorena said. "Eve is an extraterrestrial American, but she's also an angel. If you dropped your intellectual barricades and allowed your intuitive side to breathe for a minute, you'd see it's true."

Persephone raised her index finger, ready to counterargue Lorena's point. Only, she paused midbreath, then lowered her finger. She smiled. "Maybe you have a point."

"Lorena was definitely closer than you were," I said.

Eve laughed her wheezy laugh. "Persephone thought I was a special effect."

A soldier poked her head out from the cockpit. "Strap in, everyone. We're landing."

My stomach felt like I'd just hit the big drop on a roller coaster. I took a seat next to Eve and strapped in. The whine of the chopper's engine changed pitch as we started to descend.

"I don't want to do this. I'm scared, Benjamin."

I held out my hand. "I am too. But I'm less scared knowing you'll be there with me."

Eve grasped my hand. "Yes. Me too."

CHAPTER 35

I staggered out of the helicopter and wobbled down the ramp, a gusty wind messing up my freshly combed hair. Dozens of people were waiting on the edge of a big, empty field, including our classmates. They broke into applause as Eve appeared behind me.

People in uniform descended on us, two of them speaking simultaneously, one of them thanking us for our service, the other giving advice on the first thing we should say to the Alioth. Eve made a sharp, unhappy hissing noise.

Mom pushed her way into the scrum. "I want a six-foot perimeter of empty space around the emissary and her assistant, immediately."

The people who had descended on us backed off. When it came to this crowd, Mom had the power. It was cool to see.

"Benjamin!" Grace called. Lucian was standing beside her.

"I'll be right back." I touched Eve's arm lightly, then headed over to where Grace and Lucian were waiting at the edge of the crowd.

Grace immediately wrapped me in a fierce hug. "I'm so sorry about everything I said."

"I can't believe this is happening." Lucian clapped me on the shoulder. "Nice job, dude."

"We all played our part," I said. "That's why Eve wanted you here." From their beaming smiles, I could tell that meant a lot to them. Now that they knew what was happening, they wanted to feel like a part of this. I could understand that. I, honestly, wished I could be *less* a part of this.

Grace's beaming smile faded. Her mouth fell open as she looked up over my head. The field was suddenly growing shady as shouts rose around me. I didn't want to look. I wanted to see it, but I also really, really didn't.

Reluctantly, I craned my neck and gazed up.

Their ship was blotting out the sky, blocking the sun, growing larger by the second. It was a massive, multicolored jewel with a million sides, dropping lightning fast and completely silent.

One moment, it was in the sky; the next, it was parked in the middle of the field a few hundred yards from us, towering as big as a mountain. I gave Grace a pat on the back and headed back to join Eve.

"This is it." Mom kissed my cheek. "I love you."

"I love you too." Usually I felt awkward saying *I love you*, but not then.

Mom squeezed my shoulders as she let go. Beside me, Eve spread her arms. Nervous as I was, I couldn't help smiling. Eve wasn't going until she got a hug from Mom too.

Mom obliged, even giving Eve a kiss on the cheek to match mine. Then Lorena was beside me, giving me a hug as well. Then Persephone.

"Remember, they're all just people in costumes," Persephone joked. "This is all just part of the experiment."

"Don't I wish." My lips were parched again. I looked toward the crowd. "Does anyone have water?"

Before anyone else could react, Grace was there, water bottle in hand. I took a long drink, then handed the bottle back. "Thanks." It was time. There were no more reasons to delay. I looked to Mom. "What do we do? Just walk over to it?"

She shrugged. "I guess so."

I turned to Eve. She'd gone with the purple dress. I thought that was a good choice. "Ready?"

"Yes," she said.

Eve and I headed through calf-high weeds toward the ship, Eve's butterfly earrings swinging in the breeze.

"When this is over, we can play a game on my Xbox. Have you ever played Minecraft?" I asked, to break the tension.

"No."

"It's good. I'll show you when we get back." Because I was keeping the Xbox. Once we were finished saving each and everyone's butts, I figured I'd be in a pretty sweet negotiating position. *I* would have the power, you could say.

I looked up at the ship, then reached out and took Eve's hand.

DISCUSSION QUESTIONS

1. Feeling scared is never fun. *When you feel afraid, what do you do to help yourself feel better? Who are the people you like to talk to when you're afraid?*

2. After Eve hurt one of the teachers, Ben was afraid to sit by Eve at the movies. *How did Ben manage to sit next to her even though he was afraid? What are things that you can do when you feel afraid?*

3. *What does it mean to be brave? When were the characters brave? When have you been brave?*

4. For a long time, everyone thought Eve was scary and mean, but eventually Ben saw that she was really just a scared kid. *Do you know someone who acts mean? Why do you think they act that way?*

5. Because Eve had been treated so badly, it was very hard for her to trust others. *How did Benjamin, Lorena, and Persephone gain Eve's trust? How do you know when you can trust someone?*

6. By the end of the book, Benjamin has made three good friends. *How can you tell if someone is a good friend?*

7. At the end of the book, Benjamin and Eve are on their way to meet with the Alioth emissary. *What do you think happens when they meet?*

If you love *The Classmate*,
check out other spooky children's
adventures from Future House
Publishing here!

About the Author

Will McIntosh began his love affair with all things monstrous when he saw *King Kong* playing in a store while out running errands with his grandfather. Will told his grandfather they had to go home *immediately* so he could watch the rest of the movie. As a teenager, Will sold comic books at a local flea market and watched as many cheesy science fiction movies as he could. It's fair to say he didn't exactly love school—sitting still and listening is not one of his strengths—which may explain why he wrote a book about a strange school where the kids are told exactly what to say and where one of the classmates is a terrifying creature. Despite his early dislike for it, Will went on to spend years and years in school, earning a doctorate in psychology before becoming a college professor. He took up writing as a hobby in the evenings and somehow ended up working as a full-time writer. He now lives in Williamsburg, Virginia, with his wife, their middle-school-aged twins who have *way* more energy than he does, and a labradoodle named Juju.

Connect with Will McIntosh:
http://test.willmcintosh.net/
https://twitter.com/willmcintoshsf?s=11
https://www.facebook.com/WillMcIntoshSF

Want Will McIntosh to come to your school?

Will offers assembly presentations that include a 45-60 minute analysis of peeling back the secrets of successful stories. Stories like Inside Out, Wonder, Harry Potter, and countless other books and films follow the same basic story structure. Joseph Campbell recognized the pattern in myths across time and around the world. A little screenwriting book called Save the Cat transformed Hollywood by laying the secrets bare in great detail. When you see these secrets peeled back, you'll never read a book or watch a movie the same way again. Weaving together examples from contemporary middle grades books and movies, Will explores what makes a story satisfying, even life-changing.

For more information visit:
futurehousepublishing.com/our-authors/will-mcintosh

Or contact:
schools@futurehousepublishing.com